The Grits Eaters

By

Clarence L. Morrison

Copyright © 2011
by
Clarence L. Morrison

ISBN: 978-1-935802-02-0

Manufactured in the
United States of America
by

**FATHER
&
SON**
PUBLISHING, INC.
4909 North Monroe Street
Tallahassee, Florida 32303-7015
www.fatherson.com
800-741-2712

"Today I fought in the Battle of Gettysburg. I was in Pickett's charge. I wore Pat Alligood's shoes because he was too sick to fight and I had none."

**Archibald Graham Morrison, 2nd Lieutenant, CSA.
July 3, 1863.**

Archibald Graham Morrison

Amnesty Oath signed by Archibald Graham Morrison

Preface

The period following the Civil War was a frightening time for the people of the defeated South. Many historians maintain that had Abraham Lincoln not been assassinated, he would have led the South back into the Union in a more orderly manner than the harsh treatment that was administered by the semi-military government which existed following the Civil War. The cruel and ruthless treatment many southerners received following the war resulted in grave suspicions and mistrust in the national government for many years, even until today.

Many think the process of returning the South to the Union would have been quite different had Lincoln lived. The weak administration of Andrew Johnson failed to master certain members of the Lincoln cabinet. This resulted in the civilian authority having little control over the military, who forced the conspirators that assassinated the president to be tried by a military court rather than a court of civil jurisdiction.

This resulted in many questions being raised at that time and some of these questions exist to this day, almost one hundred and forty years later. Speculation existed that indicated certain members of the Lincoln cabinet could possibly have been implicated in the assassination. This theory still exists today in the thinking of many people. It was fueled by the hasty execution of the individuals who were convicted. This swiftness would lead one to consider that perhaps it was to prevent further interrogations and investigations which might have pointed the finger at individuals in high places who assumed authority following the assassination. The authority was well in excess of that delegated to their position in government by the Constitution.

In the conquered South, few individuals had a clear understanding of the events which were transpiring. In Washington, this led to little perception of the many events which would influence their lives in years to come. Soon after the armistice, the carpetbaggers and their cohorts began moving into the disorganized South to usurp the authority of the government. They further acquired the lands and properties of the people who could only rely on a very biased authority for protection.

Returning soldiers of the Confederate Army found in many instances they had nothing to return to. Many families moved west to re-establish their lives, seeking to build new homes and fortunes. Most, however, remained to rebuild their lives from the ruins they found upon their return.

The following story is a chronicle of the events in the life of a man who devoted six years of his life for the lost cause of the confederacy and the trip following his release from a federal army prison. It details the events which occurred during his journey home, what he found upon his arrival, and his life afterward. He had left an aging father and three unmarried sisters at the age of nineteen. He enlisted in the Confederate Army and in two years rose to the rank of Second Lieutenant. Following the armistice, when he refused to pledge allegiance to the United States government, he was incarcerated in a Federal Army prison for six months along with several of his men who obediently followed his lead. Finally, released with amnesty forms signed with an "X", they began the long trip home. This story reflects the events which occurred during their journey home, their thoughts, and their lives afterward.

Prologue

The weather was cold and the old man had moved a chair from the porch into the yard. There he could sit and absorb the warmth radiated by the sun in an attempt to relieve the aches in his body. As he sat watching his young children as they played, and the larger boys as they performed the chores assigned them by his wife, his thoughts reverted to the earlier days of his life and the events that had occurred in his childhood. These memories were reflected by the expressions that appeared on his face; a smile as his thoughts recovered an instance of pleasure he had experienced as a small child, and remembering the love and affection his family had bestowed him. Then a frown appeared as a moment of sorrow was remembered and he closed his eyes, refusing to relive those portions of his life that had been sad and unpleasant.

He no longer felt the strength his body had once possessed. The many harsh years of his life had drained it away and the injuries he sustained during his years of service in the Confederate Army had taken their toll. Subconsciously, he realized his time was growing short. He turned, looking toward the house, and observed his wife as she went about the task of cooking and preparing their noonday meal. She had been a faithful companion and the life they had shared had been one of the most pleasant periods of his life.

His family was the most precious thing he possessed on this earth, and he continually gave thanks to his God for these blessings. Closing his eyes he reverted to the earlier memories and began, almost unknowingly, to relive his life...

Introduction

Corn is a grain that is grown in most parts of the North American continent, from the great fields of Canada in the North to Mexico in the South. Untold millions of bushels are produced annually and much of it is shipped throughout the world to be consumed as food for people and animals, and as seed corn for future planting.

When the earliest settlers reached the North American continent, the native American Indians had grown corn and utilized it for food for many aeons and they quickly taught the settlers the art of growing this grain.

In the South, it was produced not in the voluminous abundance that was grown in the Northern plains, but the volume produced provided food for the people and their animals who had settled there. It was utilized in a number of ways, including being ground into meal and grits, and soon became a staple in the diet of those who had settled in the southern states. It is consumed today by most people of this area and my story is of the people who I know best who are the "Grits Eaters."

Table of Contents

1

The Perilous Journey
Back Home

Arch was tired. He had traveled a long way that day and was determined to reach his destination, even if it meant traveling into the night. He was going home, a place he hadn't been for six years. His perseverance grew more intense every hour of each passing day, for now he would soon be home, and then he could see Pa.

His father hadn't wanted him to enlist in the Florida Guard six years ago, and had violently opposed his going into the Confederate Army two years later, but he had believed it was his duty. He had no doubt that his father's age had influenced his resistance to him enlisting in the army. His leaving had caused hardships on his aged father and his three unmarried sisters. Now that he would soon be home, he intended to work to relieve his father from all responsibilities during the remainder of his life.

The first two years he had spent in the Florida Guard hadn't been too bad, and he learned many things about army life and the responsibilities of being a soldier. This helped prepare him for the life that followed when the Guard became a part of the Confederate Army. The company had been formed at the arsenal in Chattahoochee, Florida, and his duties had grown, especially after the Captain had selected him to be the first sergeant. It was at this time that he had to prove himself. It wasn't often a twenty-one year old man became the first sergeant of a company made up of the rough men that comprised this outfit. Many had resented him because of his youth, and only after he had proven himself and won their respect did they accept his authority. Quickly, they realized this young, non-commissioned officer from the swamps of Florida didn't give an order twice, and was capable of seeing that his orders were carried out promptly. He was tough, and while he always tried to be fair. Sometimes his methods would irritate those he saw as lazy, as these men resented being ordered to perform tasks by this young officer. When orders were not carried out promptly in an acceptable manner, it was occasionally necessary to adjust the attitude of a laggard. The young sergeant would take them away from camp and confront them physically, usually resulting in a few bruises, but promoting a different outlook by the individual who would now accept the orders given by his commander.

He was nearly six feet tall, with broad shoulders, large arms and hands, and jet-black hair. He had a ruddy complexion, browned by the sun from too many years spent outside, and piercing grey eyes, which could seemingly stare a hole through a man when the individual was being reprimanded. His years of helping his father farm in the swamp, raising hogs and cattle, had prepared him physically to perform most of the jobs he was assigned. He was proud of the confidence the Captain had placed in him when he had been promoted to the position of first sergeant. Arch had no intention of allowing a laggard to cause him to fail in carrying out his assignments. His temper was slow to rise, but when it did, no man wanted to be the one who had ignited it. His ability with a rifle was quickly recognized and this skill had been called upon several times to bring some unsuspecting Union officer to meet his master that day.

Early in the war, the company's Second Lieutenant had been killed and the Captain had asked the troops to elect a new leader. Arch was elected unanimously. At the age of twenty-two, the "Swamp Rat", as many secretly referred to him, was an officer who on several occasions had been the difference between their survival and death or capture. Some of the company said he could smell the Yankees. Often he would be called to the Captain's side to help determine a course of action that would prevent the enemy from outmaneuvering the company when in contact with the Yankee troops. His natural ability for understanding the movement of troops soon brought him the recognition of being a valuable soldier with a genuine instinct for survival.

Arch was almost home. He impatiently prodded the mule in the ribs with his heel to increase the animal's speed. He could hardly wait to see his father who he realized was getting quite old. His sisters had never married. The oldest had chosen to remain at home when her beau had wanted to marry her. She felt she needed to stay and care for their father, since he was alone and had no wife. Their mother had died before Arch's fourth birthday and now, with the disappearance of his older brother, he was the only surviving son. His two younger brothers had died when he was still a small boy, and being the only surviving son, a relationship had developed with his father seldom attained between a son and his parent. He truly loved his father who had been born in the old country, Scotland, and had come to this country when he was a very young man.

Arch's father had told of leaving his home in Northern Scotland and the grief it brought both he and his parents. Because of the harsh conditions the English imposed on the people of Scotland, he and a brother decided they should migrate to America. They had been successful in finding a sponsor after they agreed to work on his plantation for seven years to repay him for their passage. They realized when they left home they would never see their parents again. He had always longed to return, but it had never been possible. Communication with his family had been difficult and many years later he had learned both of his parents had died.

After he arrived in America, Arch's father served as an indentured servant for the seven years he had agreed to in order to repay his benefactor for his passage. His brother had slipped away and he had never seen him again.

It was during this time of servitude that his father met the woman who was to become his wife. She was the daughter of the plantation owner for whom his father worked and they quickly developed mutual feelings for one another. They were aware of their different stations in life, and knew it was an impediment that would have to be overcome if he was to be accepted by her family. This created a problem, but their strong feelings for one another remained so after he completed his period of servitude he continued to work on the plantation. He had saved a considerable amount of money before he approached the plantation owner to ask for his daughter's hand in marriage. Sadly, permission was not granted and in anger the plantation owner told him to leave or he would be shot on sight.

This did not end their strong feelings for one another. Unbeknownst to her father, he returned. Plans were made, and they eventually eloped. To avoid a confrontation with her father, they had gone far from the plantation and finally settled in South Georgia, just North of the Florida border.

Here they built a small home on land he purchased from one of the large plantations in the area. Over a period of years they were blessed with a large family. During this time, Arch's father worked diligently, and through his prudent Scottish management skills was able to increase their properties. They accumulated household furniture, farm equipment, and several farm animals including a mule, some oxen, a few cows, numerous hogs, chickens, ducks and geese. This provided a good living for the happy couple and their family. His mother's family never forgave her for eloping and she never saw any of her family again.

Fate would not let this happy family continue. Following the death of two of the younger boys, Arch's grief-stricken mother became ill and she too passed away. Arch was almost four years old, but he remembered the anguish and pains his father and the older children had suffered when his mother died. It had been a most difficult time, especially for his father, and after much praying and soul searching his father finally made the decision to move away. He couldn't stand to pass the church cemetery where his wife was buried, and following his decision to move, he spent the next two years constructing a stone crypt over her grave. Then he sold the farm, loaded his family on the two wagons he owned, and moved to Florida, which had just become a part of the United States.

It was here in Florida that Arch grew up, wandering through the swamps and pinelands, exploring the countryside, and hunting and fishing with an old Indian with whom he had become acquainted. It had been a good life, very interesting for a growing boy, sometimes hard, but for the most part enjoyable.

His family consisted of one surviving older brother who later disappeared, three sisters and a female slave his father had bought to care for his family following the death of their mother.

She never seemed like a slave, nor was she ever treated as anything but a member of the family. She had lived in the house with the family and shared their table for meals. Following the move to Florida when Pa had been away seeking a location for them to settle on, she had been left in charge of the family. Even though his oldest sister would have been capable of this responsibility, his father had chosen the slave woman. Years later she had been permitted to marry another slave from a nearby farm and it was at this time that Arch's father granted her freedom and permitted her to move away. This occurred long before Mr. Lincoln's Emancipation Proclamation was announced, which freed all slaves in the South.

As Arch rode along, he allowed his mind to wander, bringing back memories of the past and many of the events that occurred when he was growing up. He approached his father's home with the certainty of a joyful reunion and he anxiously hurried his mule along, trying to reach home as quickly as possible. It had been such a long time since he had heard anything from his family and now he could hardly wait to arrive home. He knew his family would be glad to see him and he could hardly contain himself, knowing that soon his long journey be over and he would be reunited with those whom he loved so dearly. They would soon tell him all they had experienced while he had been away.

Memories of events from the recent war flooded his mind and he recalled being summoned to the presence of Confederate General, Robert E. Lee, during the Battle of Fredericksburg. General Lee asked if he could shoot a man across the span of the river.

"Yes sir," Arch had replied.

General Lee then said, "Lieutenant, I have been told that you are one of the best shots in this army. Can you recommend another man who can shoot as well as you?"

Arch replied, "Yes sir. I have a man in my command whose ability with a rifle is fully equal to mine."

The General pointed across the river and said, "Do you see those barges being loaded with men? They are to reinforce the Union troops that have made it across the river and are systematically being destroyed."

Lee continued, "I want you to take your sharpshooter as close to the river as it is safe to approach and shoot all the gold braid you see in those three barges. Can you do it?"

Arch had responded, "Yes sir. I'll take Smith with me and we will, if possible, shoot all the gold braid we can see in those barges and any others you designate."

The General then said, "Proceed with your mission."

When he and Smith positioned themselves opposite the three barges across the river, they fired their first shots together and two Yankee Colonels toppled into the river. Quickly reloading, they shot the remaining Colonel as the barge he was on attempted to turn, and he too fell into the river. The barges quickly returned to their point of origin.

Later that day, after the battle had come to a halt, Arch was again summoned to the General's headquarters. Lee told him that the action he and Smith had performed had no doubt prevented the Union troops from achieving their goal of reinforcement and had forced them to retreat. Both he and Smith had been quite proud of their accomplishments, but now as he rode alone, he experienced deep remorse for the lives he had been required to take.

His thoughts forced him to recognize that those men had families too, and they never would return to them, but that was the misfortunes of war. Thank God, the war had ended and he would never be required to take another man's life again.

Soon Arch began to think of the carpetbaggers that would surely move into the South, and he quickly realized this might be a situation he would have to face. Hopefully it wouldn't be a problem for his family because of the remote location of their farm near the swamp. If it did surface, he would take whatever action became necessary. Few people would have designs on their sixty acres of land, but if someone did, and they tried to take any part of it, then he would fight them just as hard as he had the Yankees.

It was growing dark when Arch passed the little church and cemetery near his father's house, but the starlight allowed him to observe several graves, some of which appeared to be fairly recent. He couldn't help but wonder who the occupants of these graves could be, but soon he would learn from Pa who they were and what had caused their demise. The house wasn't too far now, only about a mile away, and his growing desire to see his family caused him to poke the mule in the ribs. The mule responded by striking up a trot, even though he had traveled many miles that day. Perhaps he, too, realized the journey was almost over and he was close to his destination where he would receive his rations for the day.

Earlier in his journey, Arch had two companions by his side. Both were men who had served under him and had also been incarcerated with him following the war and armistice. They, too, had refused to pledge allegiance to the United States government after Arch had taken his stand. They felt he had led them for four years and had never steered them wrong. Because of this, they were not going to take a stand opposing him now.

One of Arch's companions had left the group shortly after they passed near the state capitol in Tallahassee. His other companion had left him near the little town of Crawfordville, which was the county seat of his home. Arch and his companions had long before learned to avoid any populated areas whenever possible after their release from prison and to be constantly on the lookout for Union army patrols and the local officials of each town they passed. Some would be friendly, but other times they would be composed of lecherous carpetbaggers and riff-raff who couldn't wait to get their hands on other people's belongings.

Following the narrow road from the church to his father's house, he noticed that the bushes along the roadside had grown much closer to the road, something that he had never allowed when he was home. He wondered about this as he rode along and decided that perhaps Pa's age didn't allow him to perform such a task now. Well, soon he would clear the road as it had been maintained before he left. No doubt there would be many tasks for him to perform, but it wouldn't take him long to take care of such things.

Arch could soon see the outline of the house in the moonlight. It had been built on a hill near the banks of a creek that led to the river. It wasn't a fancy house like the big plantation homes he had seen in Virginia and the Carolinas, nor was it like the fancy homes he had seen in the Shenandoah Valley when they passed through on the way to fight the Yankees at Gettysburg. But it was home, the house he and Pa had built when he was a small boy. They had built the house from the large yellow pines they had cut and dragged to the home site using the oxen and mule that were usually used to plow their crops. These logs had been formed into two large rooms, connected together to provide one room to sleep in, and another with a stick and dirt chimney to keep the room warm and provide a place to cook. It wasn't elaborate, but it was tight, keeping the cold out in the winter and the cool in during the summer when the weather became hot and humid. True, each summer it was necessary to dig clay, mix it with pine straw, and re-chink the cracks between the logs. But this wasn't a big job and the time spent provided benefits that far outweighed the trouble it took to accomplish it. The roof was built using sturdy pine joists and covered with shingles they split or "rived" with a go-devil mall from the blocks sawed from large cypress logs. It provided a dry, safe home from the frequent showers that occurred during the spring and summer and the dreadful storms, which they experienced occasionally during the winter months.

When Arch arrived at the lean-to shed they used to keep the animals out of the weather, he called out loudly to the house saying, "Hey, ain't some of you people going to come out and welcome me home?"

He saw a light shining through the two glass windows, but no one answered or appeared.

He again called out loudly, saying, "Pa, it's me, Arch. Don't you want to see me? Come on out."

Following this call, a woman answered, saying, "Who are you? You better identify yourself or I'll shoot."

It was a familiar voice, but one he hadn't heard in a long time. He recognized it was his oldest sister Sarah, and he called out to her, saying, "Sister, it's me, Arch. You and the rest of the family come on out."

When the door finally opened, he saw his sister and another woman he didn't recognize. Slowly they emerged, and when they spotted him, they cautiously came toward him. Two little boys followed, peering from behind the two women. It was apparent they were afraid. He saw that his sister was holding a double barrel pistol and the other woman had an old muzzle loading shotgun, both weapons held at ready, cocked and prepared to fire if necessary. When his sister recognized him, she immediately un-cocked her pistol, handed it to the other woman, and ran to him, throwing her arms around him, crying out loudly, "You are home! Thank God! We needed you so badly."

"Where is Pa, and who is this lady with the two boys?" asked Arch.

"This lady is your father's wife, and the two little boys are your half brothers," said Sarah.

She then hesitated, and looking down at the ground said, "You don't know, do you?" She continued, "I hate to be the one to tell you, but Pa died last April. It was shortly after we heard the war had ended. He just took to his bed and a short time later he died. We buried him over at the cemetery by the church and planted a cedar tree at the head of his grave."

Pa, dead? He couldn't believe what he was hearing. It just wasn't so. No, his Pa wasn't dead. As the profound shock of what he was hearing became a reality, it was more than he could take. His knees buckled, and he fell to the ground. All these years he had looked forward to returning home and seeing his father. He had thought of working the fields for him to let him know how much he loved him, and had planned on sitting on the bank of the creek in the afternoon after a day of hard work, to listen to his father speak in his Scottish brogue. It couldn't be, it just wasn't right. He had seen many men die during the last four years, and he had caused several men to meet their maker himself. But in his wildest dreams he had never imagined that his father would be dead. Now all of his plans were for naught. He could never gaze upon his father's old wrinkled face again.

He arose from the ground where he had fallen and walked away without a word to anyone. He sat down on the creek bank, lowered his head into his hands, and began to cry.

Time passed, and when he arose from the ground, he looked into the darkened sky and from deep within his chest erupted a scream. It carried across the woods and could be heard for miles around. It echoed through the swamp in so deafening a way that the animals in the lot yard became afraid and began to move about restlessly. The chickens, geese, and the wild birds began to fly about, even though the darkness prevented them from being able to see where they were going. This scream of anguish, a hurt that couldn't be erased, reverberated throughout the swamp. It aroused and frightened the wild creatures and they, too, could be heard as they rushed about fleeing from this terrible sound that had awakened them.

To Arch, this hurt was even greater than when his side had been pierced by a Yankee rifle ball. That had been physical and it had healed, but this was something that would never heal. As he stood screaming to the high heavens, he began to see that even though he would have to accept this, it would be something he would always remember, and his regret would be that he had not been at home to minister to his father as he died.

The two women huddled together close to the house and the two little boys began to cry from their fear of the man who screamed so loudly.

"Hush! Don't let me hear any more of that," Sarah told the children.

Looking at her, their eyes wide with fear, the oldest asked, "Who is that man, big sister?"

She responded, "That is your big brother who has been off in the war. He just learned that our daddy has died and it broke his heart. Now he is getting rid of some of the pain. It won't be long before he accepts Pa's death, and then everything will be all right. He'll straighten everything out and soon we'll be getting along like we did before Pa died."

The other woman looked at Sarah and asked, "Do you think he will let me live here?"

Sarah answered, "Certainly. You can live here as long as you wish. Wasn't this Pa's house? He married you and you are the mother of his two little boys. We may not have much, but what we have will be shared by all of us. I think that is the way Pa would have wanted it."

Much later, they returned to the house. After Sarah fixed

some cold leftovers and fed Arch a meager supper, everyone went to bed.

As Arch lay in bed his mind drifted back to his life before the war and those terrible experiences where he almost died on so many occasions. He reminisced about the days he and the old Indian had successfully hunted and fished as well as the times when he sat and listened to the wise teachings by his old friend. The old Indian was now dead, but the things he taught Arch were instilled in his memory and he would need them to hunt game and face the many tasks ahead. First on his agenda was to hunt to provide some badly needed food for the family. Then the various tasks he knew that only a strong man could do would be taken in turn. As his weary mind wondered and planned about the events to come, his eyes became heavy and sleep turned into dreams of the days ahead.

2

Morning
Back On The Farm

When Arch awoke the next morning it was still dark, and only after several minutes had elapsed did he realize where he was. He lay still, then slowly stretched. He felt better than he had in a long time. Just being able to sleep in a bed again had allowed him to finally relax. The night's rest had refreshed him, and he felt prepared for the day that was fast arriving. It had been such a long time since he had slept on a bed with a sheet under him, and to know the feeling of a pillow under his head with another sheet and a quilt over him to keep the night air from chilling his body. It was wonderful, even though the mattress had been stuffed with the Spanish moss that grew so profusely on the large live oaks in the woods. When compared to six years of sleeping on the ground and in every other conceivable environment, he could find no fault with the present. To be able to lay there with the bed clothes insulating his body from the gentle cool breeze that flowed through the house was a pleasure he had only dreamed about during the years he had been a soldier. He remembered mornings in Virginia when he awoke on the ground with a blanket of snow covering the thin single blanket that covered his body, and how cold he had been. Now he was back home, and this was wonderful in comparison.

After a brief period of savoring the pleasure his bed now afforded him, he eased out quietly. Dressing quickly, he picked up his shoes and moved into the kitchen. The fire in the fireplace had gone out during the night and after searching about the room he soon located the fat-lightered splinters he knew had been brought in for the purpose of starting fires. Striking a match, he lit one of the splinters. It began to burn, at first a tiny flame and then a larger blaze that gave off black smoke as the turpentine in the splinter reached the flame. Placing several dried oak limbs from the wood box onto the fire, he soon had a roaring blaze that would quickly warm the room and provide plenty of coals to cook their breakfast. It was about this time that he heard his sister come into the room.

Looking at him she said, "We don't have any coffee and there isn't any flour, but we do have some corn meal, a little grits and a few eggs which we can cook. I'll make the meal into a pone, cook some grits and fry some eggs. I parched some corn and acorns yesterday and after I grind them up I'll make something to drink. It won't be like having coffee, but it will be better than nothing."

"Do you have any meat?" Arch asked.

"No, we haven't had any meat for several days," replied Sarah.

"I don't have any money and, even if I did, I couldn't go to the store because I have to stay here and take care of the boys."

With a puzzled look on his face, he asked, "Why couldn't their mother take care of the boys while you went to the store?"

"Well, you see," explained Sarah. "She is scared to stay here by herself and the boys are too small to walk that far and the old mule is about on his last leg, so we just couldn't go to the store. I don't know what we would have done if you hadn't come home."

"Well, cook what you have and boil that stuff you parched yesterday, said Arch. "It will be a lot better than some of the rations I lived on during the last several months. Why, sister, there were mornings I didn't have anything to eat and in fact sometimes the boys and I would go for days before we could find something we could either work for or steal. During the time we were in the Federal army prison, the food we were given was sometimes so rotten it couldn't be eaten, but then other times they would give us food that was edible. You just had to wait until they gave you food that could be eaten. Several times I strongly suspected that my stomach was convinced my throat had been cut. While we were walking home, I stole so much corn from the fields along the way that I began to think I had died, been resurrected, and come back as a hog."

"Why did it take you so long to get home after the war ended?" she asked.

"Well, you see, we didn't come straight home after the war ended," replied Arch.

"They said we had to sign a paper called an amnesty form before we could be released. This paper would forgive us for all the offenses we had committed against the United States government during the war, and, if you signed it, you would be

17

pledging your allegiance to the United States government. After spending four years of my life fighting the Yankees, I didn't think I could sign that paper in good faith. Several of my men refused also, saying if I wouldn't sign, they wouldn't either. They carried us to a prison camp in New Jersey in boxcars, and during the next six months they tried every method they could conceive of to persuade us to sign. They promised to release us, and when we still refused they used every tactic imaginable to force our signatures. It wasn't easy to refuse, but two of the boys stood by me. They said they had trusted me for four years and I hadn't led them astray. The Union army was in control of the prison, and they grew angrier every day we refused to sign. They beat us, starved us, chained us to trees in the bad weather, any anything else they could think of, short of killing us. Sometimes I think they considered doing just that, but for some reason they never did. After six months, they decided to dump us out on the road one morning in New Jersey knowing that we didn't have any money or any way to return home except to walk. I really think they thought we would starve to death before we reached home. One thing they didn't know was I had my knife and my straight razor and with these two tools we managed to survive."

Arch sat in a chair carefully lacing his worn-out shoes and watched his sister as she prepared the meager food available for their breakfast and continued, "That old black sergeant in the prison delighted in punishing me since I was a Confederate officer. When we were released, I could tell by the expression on his face that he planned to follow and kill us on the pretense that we were doing something illegal. He would probably claim we were stealing something and resisted arrest when they attempted to stop us. But he wasn't quite as smart as he thought, and his plan was foiled.

18

"After we were released that first day, we walked several miles until darkness caught up with us, Arch continued. Instead of camping near the road, I decided to go several hundred yards away in the woods which bordered the road, and we stopped by a little creek. Here we gathered wood and built a fire since we knew it would be cold that night. While we were cutting bushes to build a shelter, we spotted the old rascal and four of his henchmen, a corporal and three privates, slipping through the woods attempting to find us. Earlier we had found two old blankets in a ditch, so we placed them over some of the bushes to make it appear as if we were sleeping near the fire. We had also cut several poles and sharpened the ends to be stuck in the ground when we built our shelter. Now we each took a pole, hid in the bushes, and watched. Presently they approached, and seeing what appeared to be two sleeping forms, they all fired their rifles into them on a signal from the sergeant. We chose this time to attack, and with their rifles empty the surprise helped us overcome them. They obviously thought they could kill us with little effort, but their plan didn't work."

Pausing from the task of cooking their breakfast Sarah looked at Arch and asked, "What happened to them then?"

He gazed down at the ragged shoes he was about to place on his feet. When he finally looked up again he quietly answered, "I don't think you want me to describe what we did to them, but after you think about it and you still want to know, then I'll tell you."

Shaking her head she nodded, indicating she had heard enough, and then she asked, "What are you going to do today?"

Taking a plate, he helped himself to some of the grits along with two fried eggs and a piece of the pone she had cooked on a griddle in the fireplace. He located a knife and fork and sat down at the table. When she saw his bowed head, Sarah knew he was offering a silent prayer. He looked up afterward and said, "I thought after I had eaten I would take that Yankee rifle I brought home with me and go down to the old field next to the river and see if I could kill either a deer or a hog. If I should happen to see a bear, I guess I'll kill him because we have to have some meat. I wouldn't choose to tackle a bear, but if that is all I can find, I will. We need meat and I have killed bear before when I was a small boy and would meet to hunt and fish with an old Indian friend."

Sarah turned to him and looking directly into his eyes said, "Pa and I both knew you were meeting that old Indian, and yet this is the first time you ever mentioned him."

"Well, you know he wasn't supposed to be here," explained Arch. "He was supposed to have been sent west with the other Indians, but he was too old and couldn't have survived the trip. I have been told that many others didn't survive either. That's the reason it is called 'The Trail of Tears.' You have heard of it, haven't you?"

He then continued, "The old Indian was a good man and many of the things he taught me have served me well during the last few years. I didn't tell anyone when he died. I just carried him out into the woods near the river and buried him on a high knoll near the spot he had once shown me, where his family had been buried. I thought he would want to be placed near them and I didn't think anyone else would care what happened to him."

After he finished eating his grits, eggs and pone, he drank the corn and acorn coffee. He then picked up his hat, removed the Yankee rifle from the rack, and walked out the door in the direction of the field near the river.

3

Filling The Larder

Walking along a trail toward the riverside road, Arch could see where hogs had rooted, seeking acorns from the huge live oak trees that were abundant in the woods. He knew that hogs that fed on these acorns would be fat and would provide good meat, if only he could find a young gilt or a barrow. He realized that since his father had been too old to catch and castrate the pigs when they were young, his chances of finding a barrow were slim, but maybe he could find a young gilt that wasn't piggy and would be fat. He definitely did not want a boar since the meat would be strong. Likewise, if it was an old boar it may take several shots to kill, and he didn't have ammunition to waste.

As he slipped along trying to travel as silently as possible, he could see squirrels feeding in the trees and on the ground. He tried to avoid disturbing them and continued to move slowly, looking carefully from side to side seeking any movement that might be a game animal. He didn't see any signs that would indicate either a deer or a hog had been in the area that morning. He became severely disappointed and sat down on a stump. He cocked his ear and listened for any sound that might indicate animals feeding nearby. He heard squirrels barking as they scurried about seeking acorns to eat, and could hear crows calling in the distance, but no hogs grunting anywhere.

Silently sitting on the stump, he observed a hawk as it flew through the air, circling about to get a better view of the ground. It seemed that man wasn't the only one hunting this clear morning, but he decided the hawk didn't need food nearly as much as the man on the ground as he remembered the two little half-brothers he had left at the house who needed to be fed.

Suddenly he heard an old turkey hen yelp in the distance, and he immediately focused his attention on this sound that could mean an excellent meal or two. Slowly rising from his seat on the stump, he searched about until he found the kind of tree he sought. He pulled a leaf from a branch of the tree that was near the ground, placed it in the roof of his mouth, and began answering the turkey hen. His turkey-calling skills soon returned and the turkey began to respond. His old Indian friend would have been proud of him for remembering the lesson he had taught his little companion many years before. Soon he let the turkey do most of the yelping. Just as he began to see movement in the bushes, something moved in the edge of the field off to his right. Slowly moving his head in the direction of the sound, he saw a doe deer with her head down feeding on the little browse that grew at the field's edge. She appeared to be fat and did not give the appearance of having a fawn. The turkey had by now stepped into a clearing. She stopped to scratch and peck as she searched for food. It was now decision time and it didn't take him long to decide to shoot the doe. As expected, at the sound of the shot the turkey flew before he could reload the rifle.

The doe would provide meat for several days. Had he shot the turkey, it would have provided food for no more than two meals. He had placed the shot in the doe's neck to avoid ruining any of the meat. He walked to the dead doe and cut her throat to let her bleed. He then began field dressing by removing the head and the legs at the knee joints, leaving the skin to tie together and provide a handle he could slip over his shoulder to carry the deer home. Picking up his rifle and the deer, he started the half-mile walk back to the house.

Considering his accomplishment, it hadn't been a bad morning, for now they would have venison to eat until he could kill a hog. As he walked toward the house he suddenly thought about his father's sweet potato patch, and realized this might be another source of food that would go well with the venison. His father had always planted a sweet potato patch in the spring and no doubt he had planted one this year before he died.

If his luck held out he still might get a hog later in the day. As he walked along, he observed fresh hog signs. This meant the hogs had been in the trail after he passed earlier that morning on his way to the field. No doubt the shot had scared them, but they would be back after everything calmed down.

He decided that he would return to this area later in the afternoon, locate a good hiding place, and watch the trail in hopes that the hogs would return for another feeding that afternoon. He felt confident that he would find them feeding in the area during the next day or so.

When Arch arrived at the house, he skinned and quartered the deer and hung it in the smoke house, a small building behind the house that they used to cure hog meat in the fall.

He then located a basket and shovel and went looking for the sweet potato patch that he was sure his father had planted before he died. Just as he expected, he found the patch and began to dig the succulent tubers from the ground. With his basket full he returned to the house. He went down to the creek and washed the dirt away from the potatoes. He returned to the house by way of the smoke house, where he sliced steaks from the fresh venison ham. Carrying the liver along with the sweet potatoes, Arch presented his bounty to his sister to be prepared for their supper.

After he returned to the creek to wash his hands and face, he combed his long hair in an attempt to make his appearance more acceptable. He sat down in a chair in the kitchen and watched his sister begin to prepare the food. A sudden thought made him stand up and announce excitedly, "I think I know where there is some gold money to be found. Many years ago, Pa showed me his hiding place and told me the money hidden there was for emergencies only. I'll bet no one else knew he had the money."

Walking quickly from the house he went to the lean-to and retrieved the shovel he had earlier used to dig the sweet potatoes. He headed to the northeast corner of the lot yard and began to dig. About two feet down the shovel struck something hard. When the dirt had been removed from the object, he pulled a small metal box from the ground. Taking it to the creek, he washed the dirt from the outside of the box. He removed a small fat-lightered peg from the catch on the outside of the box, opened the lid, and removed a small leather sack with a drawstring at one end. When the drawstring was loosened a handful of shiny coins poured out into his hand. They were as bright as if they had just been minted.

Counting out ten of the coins into his hand, he handed the remainder to his sister, who had followed him. He instructed his sister to bury the rest of the coins in a new location that only she would know.

Taking the leather pouch containing the remaining gold coins she asked, "What do you plan to do now?"

"First, I am going to the creek to take a good bath and shave," Arch replied. "Then I'll go to town and buy supplies. Make a list of the things you need and let me borrow that double barrel pistol in case I run into someone who might think they need this money worse than we do."

Later, when he returned from the creek, his hair was wet and his face cleanly shaven. Using his long straight razor, he had removed the heavy beard which covered his face earlier that morning.

He began to saddle the mule he had ridden in on the previous night. Placing the McCellan saddle on its back, he secured it and placed the Yankee rifle in the scabbard. As he walked to the house his sister came out and gave him the list of supplies and the double barrel he had requested. Placing the list in his pocket he slipped the pistol into his belt, mounted the mule and rode off up the road.

4

Going To Town

The little town was about three miles east of the farm, built along the side of the railroad track and the river that flowed between the farm and the town. There was a swinging bridge about two miles north, but he knew the tide in the river would be low. Past experience had taught him that his mule could swim with little effort and apparently enjoyed the water, so he decided he would cross the river using the most direct route. He knew he might get wet, perhaps up to his knees, but that really didn't matter since the weather was fairly warm and this route would save him time.

He approached the town, which consisted of a few crude houses, such as they were, some constructed from logs and others from rough-cut lumber and mill slabs. One little store with a saloon was directly across the street. He saw there wasn't much activity going on, just a few loungers on the mourner's bench out front. This pleased him since he had no desire to talk to the few people he saw until he was able to learn more about what was going on in the community.

Pa had taught him many years before to talk little and listen to what others were saying. He said a person could learn more and reveal less by adhering to this principal. He was a wise old man, and Arch remembered his many teachings.

As he dismounted and tied his mule to the hitching railing in front of the store, he noticed the men sitting on the mourner's bench in front of the store were apparently quite curious about him. He could tell that they were looking at him, and knew they were asking one another questions about him as he finished tying up the mule. As he stepped up on the store porch, one of the men arose. "I don't believe I have seen you about before," he said, giving Arch the once-over. "Have we met?"

"No," replied Arch. "I don't expect you have seen me before, and I'm sure we haven't met." He proceeded into the store. When he looked back, he saw the man who had spoken to him resume his seat on the bench. Turning to one of the other men, he said, "I don't believe he is very talkative, do you?"

The storekeeper, an old black man, stood behind the counter. He looked up at Arch and asked, "What can I do for you, young master?"

Arch reached into his shirt pocket and removed the grocery list his sister had prepared. He handed it to the storekeeper and said, "I need the things on this list and I want a box of .50 caliber cartridges for that Sharps rifle on my mule. I need caps, powder and balls for this forty-four pistol I'm carrying. If you will, please place everything in two burlap bags so I can carry it all on my mule."

Taking the list, the storekeeper slowly read it in its entirety, and when he had reached the end he looked up at Arch and said, "I believe I have everything on your list and I'll have it all collected in a few minutes. If you wish, go outside and jaw a little with those gentlemen on the porch. I'll call you when I finish getting it together."

Arch shrugged his shoulders, indicating that he would remain inside, and the storekeeper proceeded to fill the order.

As he waited for the storekeeper to gather everything up, curiosity got the better of the men on the porch. They drifted into the store, one at a time, until they were all inside.

One of the men looked at Arch closely and asked, "Are you the son of the old Scotsman that lives across the river?"

"Yes, he was my father," answered Arch.

The man, wishing to continue the conversation, asked, "How is he getting along? I haven't seen him in town lately."

"Pa died back in April, I'm told," he answered. "I wasn't about then, but I'm back now to stay and take care of everything."

"I'm sorry to hear the old man is dead," he said. "He seemed like a good man the few times I talked with him. Are his wife and your sister still at the farm?"

"Yes, we'll be living there from now on, trying to scratch out a living," replied Arch. "I guess I'll have to raise those two little half-brothers he left and take care of his wife and my sister."

When the storekeeper had everything together, he placed it all into two burlap bags, just as Arch had requested. He then handed Arch a list of figures he had totaled, indicating the amount the supplies cost. Reaching into his pocket, Arch produced several gold coins. He paid for the items, left the store, and proceeded to tie the two bags on the mule behind the saddle. As he was tying the bags, he overheard one of the men say to another, "Why, he paid with new gold money. I wonder where he got it?"

The other man turned and said, "I don't think I'll inquire since he doesn't seem to be a talkative sort, and he might not appreciate someone prying into his business. I couldn't help but notice he was carrying a double barrel pistol in his belt, and that

Sharps rifle in the boot looks like it has seen a lot of use. I wouldn't want to rile him and add to that gun's reputation."

The other man watched Arch as he loaded the mule. "He's dressed in some of the uniform of a Confederate officer and it looks well worn," he said. "Do you suppose he was in the war?"

When Arch finished securing his purchases on the mule he mounted and turned the mule toward the store porch. The group had now moved back outside and were watching his every move. "I wouldn't want you fellows to lose any sleep wondering about me, so I'll tell you," said Arch. "I was a second lieutenant in the Confederate army and was with General Lee when he surrendered at Appomattox Courthouse in Virginia. I just got home and if nothing don't happen to prevent it I'll be there from now on. Now if any of you fellows are still curious and want to learn more about me you'll just have to come over to the farm sometime and visit. You are all welcome anytime."

With these words he turned the mule, not waiting to hear any comments from the group, and headed north. One of the men turned to the others and asked, "Why is he going north? His farm is west."

When Arch was far enough away from the store to be seen by the bench warmers, he turned the mule toward the swinging bridge. Pushing him along at a brisk pace, he quickly reached the bridge.

After dismounting and inspecting the bridge carefully, he determined it would support the mule and his load and let him cross. Remounting, he then started toward the farm at a fast pace. The sun was still above the trees and if he hurried there would be time left to hunt hogs by the field before it became too dark for him to shoot. He might get some pork before nightfall.

Arriving home, he couldn't help but notice the entire family was out under the trees, ready to welcome him home. This time when he rode in he didn't have to call out to receive recognition, for they were all eager for his return.

After he unloaded and carried the supplies into the house, he unsaddled the mule and returned him to the lot yard. Then, going to the small barn, he secured a small container of corn and two bundles of fodder. He fed these to the mule, being careful to place a bar across the opening of the stall to prevent the other animals from sharing in the mule's food.

He removed the rifle from the scabbard on the saddle. As he passed the house he called out to his sister and handed her the double barrel pistol that he had borrowed earlier when he went to town. He stopped at the well and drew a fresh bucket of water. He reached up on the post, which stood nearby, and removed the gourd dipper. After filling it, he drank, refilled, and drank a second time. He replaced the gourd dipper on the post and left, going in the direction of the riverside field.

When he was out of sight of the house he slowed his pace, moving cautiously to avoid making any noise that would warn any animals that might be nearby. About half way to the field, he stopped where he had seen the recent rooting and found a place where he could sit and watch for any animals that might wander by on the trail.

The sun was setting low behind the trees when he heard the sound of a hog grunt, and soon he could see an old sow with a litter of half-grown pigs wandering about in search of acorns. He waited, not making any sound or movement that would alert them of his presence. He was about ready to give up on seeing any more hogs that afternoon when he spotted three gilts followed by a scrawny piney woods boar as they wandered down the trail. The boar appeared to be quite interested in the largest of the gilts. Arch assumed she wouldn't be piggy and carefully shot her in the neck. This wouldn't destroy the head as he had his mouth primed for some hog head cheese. His sister would take the head and feet, clean them properly, place them in a big pot, and boil them until the meat could be removed from the bones. After cutting the meat into small pieces, she would then season it with salt, pepper, sage, vinegar, and a few other condiments he wasn't familiar with. Then, she would place it in a cloth sack that would be hung up, allowing the grease to drip out until most had been removed. The sliced pork, placed on some of that good bread she would make from the white flour he had bought that day, would make a meal fitting for even a damn Yankee.

A fire had already been placed under the pot full of water when he arrived at the house. Shortly, the water would be hot enough to scald the hog and remove the hair.

He looked at his sister and said, "Sarah, you must have been pretty confident in my hunting abilities to start the water before I returned home."

She laughed and replied, "Yes, son, I have a lot of confidence in you and when I heard the gun shoot I knew we would be needing hot water when you returned."

After he had scalded the hog and scraped it down, he hung it with the head down and proceeded to remove the intestines. He was careful to save the liver and heart. He quartered the carcass and hung it in the smoke house alongside the deer he had killed earlier. He went into the woods and returned with green limbs from a red oak, a hickory, and a sassafras tree that he split into small pieces. He started a fire with several fat lightered splinters and placed the green wood on the flame. The green wood produced a smoke, but wouldn't blaze. This smoke would prevent the flies from blowing the fresh meat until he could go to town and buy salt to cure the meat with. Once it was cured, it would be placed in a barrel for safekeeping. Now that the problem of meat was solved for a few days he could devote his time to other problems and plan for the future.

5

Inventory

While waiting for supper to be cooked, Arch wandered about the yard examining the various pieces of farm equipment recognizing many that he had used in years past. Eventually, he sat down on a log and began to plan what he must do next. He wondered if they still had cows and hogs on the open range and if those hogs he had seen in the woods were all that were left. He knew that other people could have killed or stolen the animals after his father had died leaving no one to take care of them. He had the big mule he had stolen from the Union army in Atlanta, the same one he had ridden home. This was a fine animal, strong enough to pull a plow when spring came. He had Pa's old mule that appeared to be on his last leg, but of course, his condition could be the result of not having been fed during the last few months. This could be remedied by putting him in the field, allowing him to graze on the little grass and other vegetation growing there. This, along with the corn in the barn, might be enough to restore him to a point where he would be useful again.

Then his thoughts turned to that damn jackass and the two jennies who, if turned loose in the woods, would find adequate food to sustain them. He would feed them just enough to entice them to come home at night. Maybe the two jennies would reproduce in the spring; he knew that the jackass would have bred both jennies when they came in heat. It was difficult to understand why his father had insisted on keeping these animals because they were too small to do much work, and were more of a problem then a help. But perhaps his feelings for these small animals were a carry over from his boyhood in Scotland where such animals were utilized to do farm work. He would have to watch that old jackass closely. He might cause problems should someone nearby have a mare or another jenny. Next spring, maybe someone would buy all three of the animals and any offspring they might produce. This would solve the problem.

Arch decided he would saddle the mule tomorrow and ride about to see if he could locate any cows that might be left. Those that had calves last spring should be rounded up, and the calves marked and branded before someone else decided to place their claim on them. While it would be odd if a cow with a big "M" branded on her had a calf following her with someone else's mark and brand, it had been known to happen, and sometimes the resulting confrontation didn't turn out to be very pleasant. He didn't intend for this to happen if he could help it, unless someone had already marked and branded some of his father's cows or calves.

Glancing about, he noticed they had several hens and two big roosters. He decided that they didn't need to feed two roosters, so it looked like they would have chicken and rice for Sunday dinner. If handled correctly, the remaining rooster and the hens would produce all the eggs the entire family would require. Then, in the spring, when the hens decided to set, they could raise all the young fryers they would need to fill the menu.

Watching the geese strut about, he remembered how aggravating they were. However, they did serve as good watchdogs, announcing the arrival of every person and all animals that were not supposed to be in the area. In the spring they, too, would set and later, when the goslings grew up, they could occasionally enjoy a fat goose. It had been a long time since he had tasted roasted goose and the thought of a fat goose gracing their table filled him with anticipation. Certainly no one could slip up when those geese were out wandering around the yard. Their honking would alert everyone within hearing distance when someone came about. It was true they were messy, but you couldn't have everything without some discomfort.

The more he thought about it, he decided it had been too long since he had enjoyed a goose dinner. He made up his mind to pen one up and feed it all the corn it could eat until it was fat; then they would dine on a good roasted goose again.

As he thought back he remembered the last goose he had helped eat. It had been in Virginia, when they were walking home. As they passed a farmer's house, a big gander came rushing up, hissing at them as if he were attacking. Pat Aligood had a fish hook tied to a long string. He quickly placed a grain of corn on the hook and began dragging it behind them. The old gander, seeing the dragging object, became quite interested. When he discovered the grain of corn, he grabbed the hook and swallowed it, thus becoming caught. Pat had led him down the road, the goose unable to make any noise until they were out of sight of the farmer's house. They had then killed the goose, and that night he had been the guest of honor at a most pleasurable meal that was enjoyed by all. Thinking about it made him impatient to enjoy another goose dinner.

As he again sat on his log, thinking about the situation, he realized that he had to feed two boys, two women and himself, two mules, one jackass, two jennies, about fifteen hens, one rooster (as they were planning to enjoy the other rooster next Sunday), and about eight geese. He decided he had been in much worse situations.

6

Supper

As the full moon began to rise above the treetops it brilliantly lit the clear sky, and the landscape looked as if a huge lamp had been lit to clear away the darkness and present the beautiful countryside like a picture of loveliness that only God could have painted.

Sitting on his log in the yard, Arch listened to the calling of the night birds and the frogs as they began their musical serenade of the night. It was so pleasant and peaceful to be home enjoying the wonderful sounds of his swamp. This was the place he had loved and appreciated as a boy growing up from the early days of his childhood to the present days of manhood. To again be able to sit in the yard and remember the many wonderful events of his life, recalling those times his father had counseled him and told of his life growing up in the old country. It seemed almost like something that was out of a fantasy tale. Many times, as he attempted to sleep in the distant places during the war, he had dreamt that perhaps he would be able to return home and enjoy the countryside as he was now doing. Arch remembered he often feared the next day might be his last when they engaged the enemy. He realized that he had been one of the fortunate ones and that many of his companions had gone on to meet their master. Now he could prepare himself for his future.

The daydream was broken when his sister stepped to the door and called loudly in her pleasant voice, "Supper is ready. Come and eat."

This was the most wonderful sound he had heard in many days. The invitation to come and eat immediately brought him to his feet, and he answered in a loud voice, "I am on my way." As he started toward the house, he added, "Please be sure you don't let anyone get my supper."

When he entered the room the two women and the two boys were already seated at the table. The head of the table was the only unoccupied space. Looking around as if he expected someone else to join them, he sat down. From the expression on his face his sister knew he was slightly uncomfortable sitting in this place, for it had always been their father's seat.

Sarah then bowed her head and offered a prayer of thanksgiving to the almighty God who had made everything possible. When she finished her humble prayer they began to serve their plates and soon the room became quiet and the only sound that could be heard was the scraping of their forks on the china as they emptied their plates.

The table had contained a wonderful bounty including fried pork liver, venison steak, fried ribs from the hog, grits, baked sweet potatoes, collard greens and cat head biscuits. He had looked over the table and couldn't think of anything else they needed except the sweet cane syrup which he quickly located on a shelf on the wall. It was a wonderful meal that he wouldn't forget for many years to come. When everyone had satisfied their hunger, they sat quietly, each reluctant to move, afraid to speak for fear they might break the spell that engulfed them. They had no desire to return to the reality of recent days as the past hadn't been a desirable or enjoyable period in their lives.

After what seemed like several minutes of silence had elapsed, his sister and stepmother arose and began to clear the table, being careful to place the food that remained uneaten into bowls. These containers were then placed in a screen safe at the end of the room to be consumed the next day.

While the women were occupied with their work of clearing the table and washing the plates and utensils in the kitchen, he called to the boys who still sat at the table watching him. They both looked up when he called and quickly scrambled down from the table. They came to him and stood before him. The largest of the boys asked, "What do you want, sir?"

Arch smiled and took both of them by the hand. "I just want to talk to you boys a little and become better acquainted," he said.

As their conversation continued the boys soon began to warm up to him. When they were assured he meant them no harm they quickly understood he merely wished to talk with them. Soon they began to ask him questions, some of them related to the war. Arch wished to avoid any conversation that might seem to glorify the war, so he responded by asking them questions about their lives.

Their interest in the war disturbed him. For two little boys to be interested in something so terrible was frightening. They were too young to have a fixation on something as terrible as the war, and this caused him great concern. He had gone through the war, entering it as a young, uninformed man of nineteen, and was exposed to many horrible events. He had witnessed things that he had never imagined in his wildest dreams. He observed the most raw examples of acts committed by individuals in moments of both great fear and madness. These things would never be forgotten and were certainly not justified. Should the individuals who had committed these atrocious acts against their fellow man live for another hundred years they would have to learn to live with the memories that would flood their minds in moments of quiet and reflection.

He remembered unreasonable acts others had perpetrated against him and his anger returned momentarily. He would never be able to forgive nor forget, for their actions could certainly never be justified. He sincerely hoped that in future years he wouldn't come in contact with these people who had mistreated him. While he didn't plan any revenge, he was afraid he might forget himself and commit some act of retribution that might be as heinous as those that had been committed against him. He realized that some of the acts he had committed had been terrible, but never had he been vicious or cruel. Now he faced the responsibility of raising these two little half-brothers. He knew he must never make any comment that would glorify or glamorize any part of the terrible conflict which he had participated in.

Soon, as the night began to pass, it became obvious that the boys were sleepy. When they began to nod, their mother announced it was time for them to go to bed. She accompanied them, but not before allowing each to come to Arch and say, "Good night sir." This was an indication they had accepted him as their protector in the absence of their departed father.

Shortly after they had left the room, Sarah moved her chair closer to Arch and they began to converse quietly so as not to disturb the little boys who were attempting to go to sleep in the next room. Their conversation first turned to the various members of the family. Sarah led him through the events that had occurred in his absence, and touched on each family member's life. He became quite depressed when she told how one of his sisters had died from pneumonia during the war. It seemed such a horrible thing for one's life to be ended at such an early age. She had been a beautiful woman with a pleasant smile and an active mind. All his sisters had been better educated than he. He remembered being resentful when his father had decided that each of his daughters would be sent away to be educated in the best school available, while he stayed behind and toiled in the fields. When they had received all the education available at the little church, his father had carried the girls to Savannah, Georgia and when they returned home they had taught him at night after he had finished his work on the farm. His education had been better than most of the men in his company, including some of the other officers who couldn't read or write as well as he could. He had been annoyed that his father had placed his sisters' education ahead of his, but now he understood that had his father sent him away to school he couldn't have earned sufficient money by himself to provide an education for both his son and his daughters. By sending the girls and having Arch help on the farm the girls could teach Arch when they returned. Though his father had never been formally educated, this was another example of his innate wisdom.

Arch learned his younger sister had married an itinerant Methodist circuit-riding preacher who traveled to the little church down the road, coming by about once every three months. The preacher had been a chaplain in the Confederate army and arrived home shortly after the war ended. He married Arch's youngest sister a few weeks after his father died and they now lived about one hundred miles away in an area west of his father's home. His older brother had left home before Arch had enlisted in the Confederate army, and no one ever heard from him since. His father had traveled to the place in West Florida where he was supposed to have gone, but he found no one who had ever seen or heard of him. During the years that followed they never heard anything else about him. His father died believing that his son had met with foul play and was probably dead.

Sarah was quite interested in learning about his experiences during the war and especially the period following the armistice. While Arch was still reluctant to discuss some of the events that occurred during his tenure in the Confederate army, he decided he would share with her some of the terrible things which had confronted him and his companions, and the act they had committed of which he wasn't especially proud.

"If some of the things I describe to you are too gruesome, just tell me that you don't want to hear them and I will stop," said Arch. "Maybe by telling you about some of these things I can get them off my mind and not worry about them any more."

Arch began, "After I enlisted in the Florida Guard as a private, I spent the next two years doing pretty easy duty. We watched along the coast for the federal gunboats. When they would send parties ashore to destroy the salt cookers which operated along the coast, we would attack them whenever possible. In most instances, they wouldn't put up much of a fight before they would return to their ship and sail away beyond the range of our guns. Seldom did these engagements amount to much. During this period I was promoted, first to corporal and then to sergeant. Later, when the company was formed at the arsenal at Chattahoochee, I was selected by the captain to be the first sergeant of the newly formed company. Many of the men in this new company didn't like the captain's choice, but I soon convinced them that I was man enough to handle the job. At times I would have to take a man out into the woods away from the camp for an attitude adjustment. Sure I would whip them, and soon they knew I was damn tough and man enough to be their first sergeant. Others didn't care to try their hand at unseating me, and soon there was no dissension among the men of my company. I was the first sergeant and what I said was carried out promptly from that time on. I was proud of my job and the confidence the captain had in me when he appointed me to the position. Working hard, I soon had the company molded into a real fighting group."

Arch continued on.

"About that time we were moved to Lookout Mountain in Tennessee. Shortly after we arrived there the second lieutenant was killed during one of the first battles we were engaged in. The captain called the men together and told them to elect a new second lieutenant, and I was chosen unanimously. I served in that capacity during the remainder of the war and was discharged as a second lieutenant. The discharge came from the Union army when I was released from the Federal army's prison in New Jersey."

Arch went on, "Once, while I was in Tennessee, I was sent to West Florida to pick up uniforms for our troops. The train ride through the Smokey Mountains was an experience I will never forget. They were so beautiful, with the colorful flowers in full bloom, and the different shades of green reflected in the mountainside trees. It was a very pretty sight for a country boy who had never traveled much during his life."

Of course, Arch didn't describe to Sarah the encounters he had with the lovely Tennessee ladies who had been very nice to him when he was on leave. Such things one didn't talk about, especially to their sister, but they had been wonderful experiences that he would remember to his dying day. He thought about a young widow who had become quite amorous when he had accepted her invitation to accompany her to a dance. He had never before experienced anything like what happened to him that night and he would remember and treasure this memory forever. Perhaps sometime in the future if he ever accumulated sufficient funds he just might return to the mountains and try to relocate the lady who had made such an impression on him.

Arch remembered the many attempts the Union army made to dislodge the Confederates from their stronghold on Lookout Mountain. They were never successful in their endeavor while his company was stationed there. Later, after his company had been transferred to Northern Virginia, they were able to remove the Confederate army from the mountain.

Union General George McCellan, President Abraham Lincoln's commanding general, was threatening to capture the Confederate capitol at Richmond, Virginia, and Arch's company had been moved to help put a halt to this endeavor. From this point on, Arch had participated in every major battle that occurred in the war. He didn't stop until he stood in the ranks as his General, Robert E. Lee, made his last trip past the troops at Appomattox after surrendering to General Grant on April 9, 1865.

Arch looked at his sister with tears in his eyes. He described this time of surrender that had been the most heartbreaking experience he'd had to endure during the entire war. He'd had to witness the humiliating experience of surrendering at Appomattox, and then had been incarcerated by the Union army for refusing to pledge his allegiance to the United States Government. Lastly, he'd had to promise to never take up arms against the United States again. It had truly been a terrible experience for him. True, he had been wounded three times, but this was much more painful than any of these wounds. To witness his General offer his sword to General Grant, who refused it, and then to see a lieutenant grab it instead, had been so upsetting for him that had it been possible to get his hands around that man's neck there would have been one less Yankee to return home.

Under the terms of the surrender, officers of the Confederate army were allowed to retain their side arms and horses. Since Arch had refused to take the Oath of allegiance, he was not given the same terms. He had neither a horse nor side arm, so he surrendered his rifle but kept his razor and pocketknife hidden.

To receive a discharge, each man had been required to sign an amnesty form pledging their allegiance to the United States government, and were to promise to never rebel against the government again. This had been something he just couldn't bring himself to do, and when he refused, several members of his company refused as well. Those who refused to sign were loaded into boxcars and carried under guard to an army prison in New Jersey.

Arch told Sarah that it was there he was forced to endure the most pitiless treatment he received during the entire war. Each day they were awakened long before daylight and were forced to stand at attention outside, regardless of whether it was raining or clear. Sometimes this would last several hours and if a man broke rank or even moved without an order, he was immediately dragged to a whipping post and flogged severely. Later, they would be marched before a Union officer seated in a covered area behind a table. Each man would be asked his name and if he had changed his mind and was ready to sign the amnesty form pledging his allegiance to the United States government. Some would be unable to endure the torture any longer and would sign, only to be seen no more. It was assumed they had been released, but no one was really sure what happened to them. Those who continued to decline the invitation to sign would then be marched back to the prison and their treatment would begin again.

The Union troops were under the direction of an old black sergeant who had at one time been a slave. He would direct his men each morning to administer their punishment so that marks wouldn't show, and then instruct them to begin the daily ritual. This was the signal for the prisoners to be whipped and subjected to the most degrading punishment the Union soldiers' simple minds could conceive. Many times they would be taken outside if the weather was bad and tied to trees. Their food was pitiful, sometimes containing bugs and worms, and even the remains of vermin. There was never enough food, such as it was, and for further punishment they were denied clean water, only filthy dirty water which no doubt contained the pollution of the camp. Their treatment had been indecent, and the suffering, disease, and death that resulted reflected the lack of integrity of the troops who now were their masters.

It seemed to delight the old black sergeant to administer the whippings to Confederate officers, and on several occasions he had been so diligent in his task that men died from the shock of the experience. Some of those who suffered his whippings thought that perhaps he was reliving some of the treatment he had received prior to his freedom from slavery. Arch knew his sister could see the hatred he had for this individual.

"I made up my mind that if almighty God permitted me to survive and I could locate that man I would hasten his departure from this earth," he said.

"I prayed that his next meal would be in the pits of hell as a guest of the devil himself.

"On the day of my release, " Arch continued, "along with two of the men from my company who had followed me throughout the entire war, it became apparent the old sergeant had not been aware such action was forthcoming. His displeasure was clearly reflected by his actions, and he became very surly when the announcement was made."

Arch paused briefly, then continued on.

"It had been early in the morning and a new camp commander had arrived the night before with orders to clear the prisoners out, even if it meant signing their amnesty forms with an "X". The prisoners were told to pack their meager belongings, line up, and march to the camp gate. There, each man received his amnesty form signed with an "X" and was then released.

"Fortunately," said Arch, "both myself and my two companions were in fair physical condition, considering the treatment we had received in the army prison. Being suspicious of the motives of the Union army, and fearing that we were being prepared for some type of further punishment, we left quickly, even though we had no money and no idea how we would return home. Before we left we saw the expression on the old sergeant's face as he talked to four of his cohorts who had always been eager to administer any type of punishment to us prisoners. It was apparent they were planning something, and we were well aware it wouldn't be in our best interest.

"After leaving the camp," continued Arch, "we talked amongst ourselves, trying to determine what had motivated our release. We noticed something in the ditch and discovered it to be two worn blankets that had been discarded. Apparently prisoners who had been released earlier had decided to abandon them, and since we had no blankets, we decided they might come in handy during the cool nights ahead.

"We walked several miles that day and as night approached we began to look for a place we could camp. We left the road and walked several hundred yards into the woods. We soon came to a small, clean creek with clear, cold water. We cut bushes from the banks and fashioned them into a lean-to that afforded come comfort while we slept. After first clearing out a place, we gathered firewood for the night. We then proceeded to cut several poles and some bushes. It was during this time that we discovered the old sergeant and his men had tracked us and were searching the woods, trying to discover our camp's location."

At this point, Arch told Sarah of the attempt the sergeant and his cronies made to murder he and his companions. Sarah listened quietly until Arch reached the end of his story.

"The many months of torture which these men had

administered to their prisoners and the visible delight they had enjoyed in beating their wards now fueled our tempers, igniting the severe action which followed," explained Arch.

"Before any of us could think rationally, we beat the former guards to death. The old sergeant had revived enough to realize what was happening, and began to beg for mercy, but we had no mercy for him that night. No doubt the many times he had tortured others while they begged for mercy now flashed through his mind as my long, straight razor approached his throat. As his head was almost severed from his body, he emitted a bloodcurdling scream as if he had seen the front gates of hell opening to allow Satan to welcome his unworthy soul into eternity. At last I had been able to carry out the revenge I had so long planned for the treatment I had received at the hands of this man and his cohorts.

"After the last soldier had been killed, it became very quiet. We soon realized the seriousness of what we had done," said Arch quietly.

"We had killed five Union soldiers and if our actions were discovered it would mean a quick trial and our execution." Arch continued, "The sergeant and his men had not been sent to kill us by their superiors. They were carrying out the desires of the sergeant who no doubt did not want anyone to survive who could tell of the treatment and events that had occurred in the prison camp. Now we had to dispose of the bodies and their equipment. We saved only the cash money we found on their bodies. We buried everything else, including their guns. We scattered leaves and other debris about the ground to hide all signs of what had occurred and what now lay beneath the soil. We wanted to remove any trace that would cause anyone to suspect what had happened on that spot."

Sarah had watched the expressions on Arch's face as he related the happenings of the past years. She had observed the changes that occurred as he related his memories of the difficulties he had encountered. It had been difficult for her to remain silent and not ask questions, but she did not wish to break his chain of thought as he described the events in his orderly and detailed manner. Arch finally paused, looking up at the clock on the wall. He noted the time and realized he had talked late into the night. At this point, Sarah stood up to excuse herself for the night. Arch worried that he might have said too much, that he might have upset her with the grisly details of his tale.

She said, "Son, you don't know how wonderful it is to have you back home. Perhaps we can resume this conversation later and you can explain some of the things you mentioned tonight."

"Yes," Arch answered.

"I am so glad to be home and proud that we can now work together and make a life for ourselves. My only regret is that Pa isn't here to guide us. It looks like you and I will have the responsibility of providing for those two little boys now that he is gone."

After Sarah left the room, Arch continued to sit at the table, staring down at the hands that had so violently taken the life of the Union sergeant. His thoughts returned to that night, and to what had occurred afterwards.

When their task had been completed, Arch and his companions reached a decision to remove themselves as far from the scene of the incident as was possible. They began walking again, although they were worn out from the distance they had already traveled earlier that day. Fueled by the excitement of the engagement, their bodies seemed to develop new energy. Instead of returning to the road, they walked in a westerly direction, being guided by the stars and the bright moonlight that permitted them to move easily as they had many times in the past, during the war. Just before dawn, they approached a road leading south. However, since they were now exhausted and badly in need of both food and rest, and not knowing what might lay ahead, they decided to lay up for now and resume their movement when it became dark again. Soon, they located a place that would permit them to watch the traffic on the road.

It became obvious they had to have some food, so Arch cautioned his companions to remain hidden while he scouted about for something they could eat. He located a farmhouse nearby and Arch slipped into their garden after making sure they didn't own a dog. He was able to find several different vegetables, including tomatoes, cucumbers, a small watermelon, and some sweet corn. He tried to remove the vegetables without leaving any signs behind. That way if an army patrol should happen to stop by and begin asking questions, the farmer wouldn't have any indication anyone was nearby. Returning to their camp, Arch and his two companions ate the fresh vegetables. One always remained alert while the other two would sleep.

Several times they observed army patrols and other traffic on the road. Once a patrol had stopped so near they could hear the conversation of the troopers as they relieved themselves. They were discussing the missing men, and it was obvious they were searching for them. They mentioned a sergeant, a corporal, and three troopers who were absent without leave. It was the patrol's opinion that it would go very hard on the sergeant since he was regular army, not one of the conscripts like the other four. Little did these troopers know that the quarry they were seeking would never be brought back for a trial, and Arch hoped fervently that they would never be located.

The officer who was in charge of the patrol was a captain. He told his men they would return to camp since they had not seen any indication the deserters had come this way. This had been good news for Arch and his fellow travelers. Now this patrol wouldn't be out looking for anyone that night, and since they hadn't located any evidence of their quarry in the area perhaps no other patrols would be searching along this road. When nightfall came, Arch and his friends resumed their trek towards home.

During the next few weeks they confined their traveling to the nights, sleeping only during the day. Always on the alert when traveling, they avoided towns and communities. They were especially careful to avoid farmhouses where a dog could be heard barking. This resulted in precious time being lost, but it helped them avoid any confrontation. Only when they passed a farmhouse and no one was aroused, nor did they see or hear a watchdog, would they raid the farmer's garden. Any vegetables they found would be eaten raw since they didn't have any method to cook.

One day providence smiled on them as they found a small iron pot. Now when they were able to steal corn from the many fields they passed they could boil the roasting ears and have a feast. Once while they were boiling some corn they had just stolen, a man came upon them. He was the owner of the field where the corn had come from.

When he observed the pitiful condition of the men, he asked, "Would you men like to accompany me home and have a good meal?" He continued, "You could sleep in my barn tonight on the hay. This would be much better than sleeping out here in the woods. I know this isn't much to offer, but it is the best I can do."

At first Arch and his men were reluctant to accept the offer, being suspicious of his motives, but after talking with the man for a little while the thought of a good meal soon outweighed their suspicions and they agreed to accept his offer. They planned to keep a watch that night just in case this man had some ulterior motives.

After they arrived at his small farm, Arch and his companions washed and cleaned up. Soon the man's wife, a large woman, served them an abundant meal of several vegetables seasoned with cured meat, and a dark bread which tasted delicious. During the night, one of them remained awake at all times while the other two slept. By maintaining a constant surveillance of the house, they were assured that none of its occupants would leave and alert the authorities of their presence. They left the next morning before daylight, while the couple still slept. They left a note expressing their gratitude and thanking them for the kindness that had been extended to them.

7

On The Road South

Time passed slowly. Days became weeks and weeks became months as they slowly moved toward their first objective, Atlanta, Georgia. It was apparent that winter was fast approaching. Traveling was slow in their weakened condition. Occasionally, while they walked during the daylight hours, which they could do now that they were in the South, some farmers would permit them to ride on their wagons or ox carts. The wagons made good progress, but the ox carts were slow. There was no appreciable increase in their progress, although it did rest them physically.

Once a farmer who had given them a ride on his wagon asked if they would like to accompany him the short distance to his home. He had become quite friendly as they traveled and soon began to sympathize with them. He made the offer when they reached the road to his farm.

"It's only a short distance up this road and you could lay over a few days and rest," said the farmer. "We could feed you some good country rations and I suspect this, combined with rest would do you a lot of good and prepare you for the remainder of your trip. "

After discussing the offer amongst themselves, they accepted and stayed several days, recuperating and enjoying the nourishing food the farmer's wife served them. They attempted to repay the couple by assisting with the chores and other tasks that needed to be done. Soon the couple quit starting new projects, only performing chores that were absolutely necessary. They knew the former prisoners should rest and regain their strength if they intended to walk the rest of the way to Florida, which was still several hundred miles away.

In a few days, refreshed from the rest and the rehabilitating food, they resumed their journey. It was difficult to leave these kind-hearted people who had opened their home to them and provided the best treatment anyone had offered during their trip.

After what seemed like an eternity, they approached Atlanta. The terrible devastation and destruction they observed was both shocking and sickening. Much of the city had been destroyed and they soon realized that the troops under General Sherman had destroyed several large portions of the city that did not have any military value whatsoever. This was the misfortunes of war. They soon realized that had the Confederate army been successful in their invasion of the northern cities, no doubt much of this same type of havoc would have been extended to any city that had attempted to stop the advance of a Confederate army. Sadly, much of the destruction appeared to have been unnecessary. They now began to wonder if the remainder of the South had suffered the same terrible destruction they were observing here in Atlanta.

After looking about for a place, they chose a location near a corral. The Union army had established this some distance from habitation to provide a secure area in which to confine horses, mules and a few cattle that ran wild following General Sherman's infamous march through Atlanta and on to the sea. Here, they could be detained until some disposition could be made. Arch and his companions noted that only one Union soldier provided the security for the area and this post was changed only once each twenty-four hours. The guard change was made each afternoon around six o' clock. They speculated that this might provide the opportunity they needed to acquire transportation for them to reach home more quickly than walking the remaining distance. It would mean stealing at least three or four animals from those confined in the corral. Four would provide an animal for each man and a pack animal to carry the supplies they hoped to obtain. Before they gave the idea serious consideration, they would have to solve their most pressing problem of finding enough food for the remainder of their trip. When this problem had been solved, they would worry about the horses. Each day their thoughts returned to the confined animals. They hoped that no disposition of these animals would be made before they had the chance to steal a few.

The food problem was soon solved when a kindly old gentleman approached them with a proposition to furnish them food in exchange for work. This opportunity seemed too good to be passed up and they mutually agreed to work for seven days in exchange for adequate food to sustain them during their employment. When the seven days were up, he would give them the food they needed for their journey home. Each day they worked from early morning until late in the afternoon and each afternoon the old man would give them a small amount of flour, salt, corn meal, cured meat and a little coffee. The seventh and final day, they completed the assigned work in the afternoon and when they arrived at the old gentleman's home they were met by a black women who they assumed was his maid or cook.

She informed them that their employer had gone to Savannah, Georgia and wouldn't be returning for several months. When they asked if he had left anything for them she informed them he had not. Sorely disappointed and extremely angry, they left and returned to their camp.

As they prepared their afternoon meal they discussed the situation, cussing the old man constantly. Finally, after long hours of pondering over the matter, a decision was reached and a plan devised.

Each day when the old man had given them their food he had gone to a barn-like building in the rear of his home. After unlocking the door, he would go inside, leaving them to wait until he returned with the promised food. This building was obviously the storehouse that contained his supply of food, so the old bastard would be surprised when he returned to discover they had collected their wages on their own. He had not intended to live up to the bargain they had agreed to originally, but they would see that his end of the agreement was kept that night.

Late in the night, after the moon had gone down, Arch and his companions approached the dark house. It appeared to be unoccupied. Going to the rear of the barn-like structure, they tried each window and door but found none of them open, so they pried loose several boards. They entered the interior of the building. Being careful not to make any noise, they soon found the barrels that contained the corn meal and flour and removed the amount they had been promised. Hanging in an area which was walled off to serve as a smoke house, they found hams, shoulders, and sides of cured meat. Nearby was a coffee mill and several lard cans of roasted coffee beans, along with cans of salt and sugar. When the amount of food they had been promised was collected and placed in burlap bags, they left, being careful to replace the boards they had removed. Unless someone looked very carefully, their intrusion would not be detected.

Arch told his companions, "I only wish I could run into the old bastard one more time. I think I would introduce him to Mrs. Sharp. " Both of his companions knew he was referring to that long straight razor he always kept in his shirt pocket. Many times they had discussed that razor, wondering where Arch had acquired such an instrument, and how he kept it so sharp.

The next day they rested all morning, going over their plans to steal the four mules they had already picked out. They waited patiently until after the guard change that afternoon before making their move. They had asked several other Confederate soldiers who were camped nearby if they would gather at the end of the corral at the furthest point from the guard's station. They were to create a disturbance to divert the guard's attention. While this was going on, Arch and his two companions would slip up behind the unsuspecting guard and mug him. They had no intention of hurting the man, only render him incapable of sounding an alarm or interfering and preventing them from stealing the four mules.

Everything worked out exactly as had been planned. While Arch tied and gagged the guard, the other two caught the mules and began to saddle three after they had secured their supplies and other belongings on the fourth mule. When Arch returned, he was carrying the guard's gun, a .50 caliber rifle and the ammunition pouch, knowing full well that if he were caught he would be promptly hanged. His desire for the gun was worth the risk, and they had already committed enough offenses which would warrant their execution if caught. Arch told his companions, "What the hell? They cain't hang you but once, so what have we got to lose? If we are caught, I plan to send a few of the blue bellies to hell with this gun before I die."

As they were leaving they called to the other Confederates

who were watching and told them, "Help yourselves." They knew full well that when the next guard change occurred not a single horse or mule would remain in the corral. All they would find was a tied up guard who would have suffered through the long period that would pass before he was discovered. The Union army would have many trails to follow after they discovered what had happened. Perhaps they wouldn't be pursued, but if they were, the trail would be many hours old.

Skirting the main parts of Atlanta, they were careful to avoid any route that might result in an encounter with the Union army patrols. By dawn the next morning, they were many miles south, and getting closer to home as each hour passed. While there were Union outposts in nearly every town of any size, they still found people who were sympathetic to their plight, and warned them when they were in danger of encountering the Union army patrols. Those people would often hide and feed them until the danger of being discovered had passed, and sometimes serve as guides helping Arch and his companions avoid those roads that were constantly being patrolled. They showed them short cuts around towns and provide other information that might be helpful. Occasionally they would be required to hide in someone's barn for a day or two when efforts of the Union army were intensified. The further south they progressed, the stronger support they received from the populace and now it appeared they would soon be home. It had been so long since any of them had heard from home, and they constantly wondered what had happened to their families. Each anticipated a most joyous occasion when they reached their long sought destinations. These thoughts were always on their minds and this fueled their eagerness to reach home as quickly as possible.

At night, when they camped in the woods away from the roads, they would sit around the fire and discuss the different battles they had participated in, sharing their experiences. In all of these discussions, no reference was ever made to the events that had occurred on the day they had been released from prison. It was like a bad dream which none of them had any desire to reflect upon. The terrible acts they had been forced to commit haunted them, but each handled his problems in his own way, never imposing his guilt on his companions.

Sometimes, Arch's companions noticed him sitting and staring into the fire, brooding and reliving events of the past. These memories were so horrible that he couldn't dismiss them from his mind. From the expressions flickering across his face, it appeared that he was reliving a battle and the actions he had performed. He would be transfixed, his face reflecting fear, joy, sorrow and anger. His companions never tried to talk to him during these times, for they, too, had their share of these moments and they understood his pain.

Arch was always kind to his companions and only occasionally spoke to them in a harsh manner when something they did or said irritated him. Both of his companions accepted him as their leader, and the relationship that evolved amongst them was something that is seldom achieved between individuals. It couldn't easily be explained, but it developed so strongly that it would continue throughout their lives, and no action by any of them would weaken this bond. Many years later an event would occur that would test the strength of this bond, and it would be found to be just as strong as when it evolved. The only thing that would terminate the connection between these three men would be their death.

The closer they came to their homes the stronger their desire became to see their loved ones. They constantly wondered how their families were living and how they were coping with the hardships they knew were facing them.

Soon they became careless. Arch took it upon himself to once again remind them of the importance of always being watchful so as to avoid being captured by either a Union patrol or some of the local officials of the areas they were traveling through. These local officials were composed mostly of riff-raff, carpetbaggers, freed slaves and the traitors of the South who had refused to support the Confederate government. Such people would show them no mercy if they were caught. No doubt they would be hanged on the pretext they had either committed some crime or were attempting to commit some act against the local government. Their animals were branded with a big "U S" which indicated they were property of the Union army and probably stolen. This would be all the evidence such people would need to justify hanging them. Through contacts with some of the locals they had been able to trust, they had learned of terrible acts that had been committed against residents by some of these unscrupulous people. They knew they needed to move carefully, and only when they were sure they could avoid those who now controlled the local governments. Long ago they had agreed to resist as strenuously and fearlessly as possible if they should be approached by one of these groups, knowing that the one rifle was the only weapon they possessed.

Only once did Arch and his companions encounter any of these people, and the threat they posed was quickly dispelled when the intruders realized these three would not be easy prey. These had been only six in the group. They were on horses and being lead by an individual who apparently had never encountered any resistance. Unsure whether these three would surrender or fight, he had displayed indecisiveness. This indicated he was not sure of himself, and his questionable actions confirmed this.

Stopping some distance away, the men watched Arch and his two companions, and saw that they appeared to be armed and ready. From a safe distance, the group asked Arch and his fellow travelers if they would like to join them. When their offer was declined, they quietly rode away without giving them any problem or further trouble. The guns they thought they had seen had been only the one gun Arch had stolen from the guard, and two pine poles they had cut and fashioned to look like guns from a distance. The ploy had worked, and as the men rode away, Arch and his companions couldn't help but be amused by their own wit.

They came to an area near the Florida/Georgia border that Arch remembered as a child. This was where he had been born and raised the first few years of his life. His mother was buried at the little church, and he asked his companions to stop long enough for him to visit her grave. Neither had any objection, and both accompanied him to the grave site. Later they stopped at the house where Arch was born. After conversing with the current residents he learned that some of the people he remembered from the area had moved and now also lived in Florida. One person who he specifically remembered was a man who he was told had settled in the part of Florida near where his father had located. He filed this information away, and planned to look this man up when he arrived home. This individual had been a staunch supporter of his family, even to the point of helping his father on several occasions when the old man couldn't accomplish certain tasks without help from someone else. Arch planned to offer to assist him in some of his work as repayment for the kindness he had shown his father.

Late the next afternoon they reached the outskirts of Tallahassee, the capitol of Florida, which really wasn't much of a town. They observed that it was absent of the signs of war being fought there. They later learned that this was the only state capitol east of the Mississippi River that the Union army failed to capture. They noticed Union soldiers patrolling the area, but were not approached or questioned. They decided the

61

war hadn't reached this region as there were no signs of the devastation they had seen in Atlanta.

Shortly after they passed through Tallahassee, Pit, Arch's companion from Jefferson County, decided to leave the group. His home was to the southeast, and to continue with Arch and Pat would be out of his way and would only make his trip longer. The decision to leave his companions who he had been with for all these years, the ones who had suffered with him during the many trying times, was a very difficult one to make. But his ever-growing need and intense desire to see his wife and children overrode his reluctance. After a final handshake and many promises had been made did he turn his mule in the direction that would be the most direct route home. The men parted with tears in their eyes.

The remainder of the trip was uneventful, and the two remaining travelers parted company later that afternoon near the county seat. It was a little community composed of nothing more than a wooden courthouse and a few dwellings, with two stores and a print shop. Again it was with sadness that these two parted company, and now Arch continued his quest to reach home and see his father.

Pat had offered to accommodate him for the night, but his desire to reach home and see Pa was too great for him to stop and delay their reunion. The few miles that faced him would be covered long before midnight. With tears in their eyes they said good-bye, and now Arch was alone. He prodded his mule, anxious to cover the remaining miles as quickly as possible, for he just couldn't wait to see Pa. It had been so long and now it appeared he would soon be home.

8

The Round Up

Early the next morning, immediately after he finished his breakfast, Arch saddled his mule and began the round up of all cattle he could find bearing his father's mark and brand. His father had always branded his cattle with a big "M" on each cow's right hind quarter. This distinguishing brand, accompanied with an earmark of a swallow fork in the right ear and a crop on the left ear, clearly identified the owner of each cow. The round-up required several days of hard riding, searching the woods for miles around to locate the animals which had wandered away seeking good grazing. The piney woods provided wire grass, but the cattle would wander about seeking new growth that resulted from the woods fires which Arch knew the different cattle owners set in the early fall to encourage the grass to grow early. Cattle would find these burns and feed in these areas until they had consumed the early growth, leaving only the tough range grass that remained to grow to maturity.

Soon he had a large herd of cattle rounded up and penned. While he was confident he had the majority of his father's cattle, he realized he would locate more after he had branded and marked the ones he had rounded up. He then began the hard work of marking and branding the calves that followed the older cattle. To mark and brand the larger of these animals was a big job and he really needed assistance, but since he didn't have anyone to help he would have to accomplish it alone.

Remembering how he had seen it done by northern farmers who had larger animals to handle, he built a pen using pine poles. On one side he built a narrow break with a gate inside the pen to close the break. He placed another gate at the other end of the break with a hole in it that would be big enough for a cow to stick their head through. He then anchored a pole in the ground that would pivot to a vertical position when it was pulled to the side, thereby reducing the size of the hole. When an animal attempted to escape, they would stick their head in the hole. When he pulled the pole against the animal's neck it would prevent the animal from backing up or going through the hole in the gate. He would then secure the pole against the animal's neck and proceed with the branding and marking. However, when it was a bull calf he would take a short rope and tie it to the animal's tail. He would then pull the tail up over the animal's head and secure the rope to the fence. With the tail tied in this manner the animal couldn't kick, and Arch could then proceed with the job of converting the bull to a steer. To avoid the possibility of an infection or screw worms, Arch coated the incision with gum turpentine that was collected by skinning a pine tree and cutting a gash, allowing the gum to run. He knew the gum would blister the raw exposed cuts and no doubt cause great pain to the animal, but it was necessary because he didn't have time to be catching calves to treat screw worms. It was a slow job for one man, but during the next several days he would rise early and return late each day, completely exhausted, but with a satisfying sense of accomplishment. Each day as he marked and branded the cattle, he diligently maintained a record of each animal, being careful to write down a description of each. He was proud when he realized he had twenty-three grown cows, fifteen mixed calves and two grown bulls. He planned to capture and castrate one of the bulls when he could find someone to assist him. This was too much of a job to accomplish by himself. In the meantime he would watch the bull and make sure no one else tried to brand him with another brand.

There were plenty of hogs in the swamp, so he built a trap, baited it with corn, and caught several hogs each night. He released the sows and pigs after they had been marked and the boars castrated. When he caught a fat barrow, he would kill it for meat. The thinner ones were placed in a pen and after being fed corn for a few weeks, they too were butchered. Soon the smokehouse contained meat sufficient to feed the family throughout the winter and spring.

Now he began the job of clearing the fence rows and repairing the fences where necessary. Soon he would begin breaking the ground in his fields to make them ready to plant immediately after Easter Sunday. His father had taught him to wait until after Easter to plant since it seldom got very cold after the holiday. This was his plan for the next year subject to changes he couldn't anticipate now.

Once when he was returning home after a day of repairing fences, he heard loud talking in the direction of the house. When he got closer, he saw a man talking loudly, gesturing with his hands, demanding that his sister and stepmother leave immediately. Cursing, stomping his feet and waving his hands in a threatening manner, he told them he would do them bodily harm if they didn't leave the farm.

He was a big man, neatly dressed with polished boots and a big felt hat. His horse, tied to a bush nearby in the yard, was a fine animal and his saddle and bridle would lead one to think this man was a man of financial means. Arch heard him say, "I am going to run you squatters off this land and I plan to live here myself. I don't need you rednecks living here messing up this place. Do you hear me, you old bitches?"

The man wasn't aware that Arch had approached and was listening to his boastful and derogatory remarks to the two women. When he turned and saw Arch standing there with his rifle in his arms, his attitude changed immediately, becoming quieter and lowering his voice. When he spoke again it was directed to Arch. Stammering, he said, "I didn't know you were there. I was just telling these ladies that I had bought this property and they would have to leave."

Arch just smiled, but the expression on his face reflected the fire that had been ignited by this man. The man saw this and became afraid, realizing Arch would hurt him if he got close enough. Then he saw that Arch was holding a rifle, which made the situation more frightening. Arch said quietly, "Mister, I don't know who you are, and frankly I don't give a damn, but this property was bought by my father a long time ago from the federal government, and if I ever catch you on the west side of the Sopchoppy River again I'll feed you to a gator. Now my advice to you is to apologize to the ladies, get your stinking Yankee ass on that horse and ride out of here as fast as he can carry you because the longer I see your sorry face the madder I get. In just about one more minute I am going to shoot your damned head off. Do you understand me?"

Before Arch could finish, the man realized he had made a terrible mistake coming to this farm; it wasn't like the others he had approached. This man would hurt him, if he didn't kill him. He quickly tipped his hat to the ladies, backed away from the front door, and grabbed the reins of the horse. As it began to move, he mounted hurriedly, crouching low in the saddle as if he expected to be shot in the back. Without looking back, he rode away in a gallop.

As the rider disappeared, Arch turned to his sister and quietly said, "Don't you ever let any carpetbagging son-of-a-bitch talk to you like that again. If it ever happens again just take your pistol and shoot the bastard. I'll get rid of him when I get home and no one will ever know what happened."

With these words he turned and disappeared in the direction of the barn, proceeding with the task he had previously planned. He anticipated an event like this would happen, but that one wouldn't be back if he knew what was good for him. He really wasn't ready to start anything at this time, there was too much to do, but he didn't plan on avoiding this kind of trouble for if he did, then others would think they, too, could impose on them.

Weeks later, nothing had been heard from the man he had run away. Arch was certain that word had gotten around that their farm wasn't up for grabs, and anyone who had designs on it should be prepared for trouble.

As the weeks passed, his fields began taking shape and Arch decided they would be ready to plant immediately after Easter. He always remembered the advice his father had given him. Wait until after Easter to begin committing your seed to the ground. His father's knowledge had been gained over a lifetime, and Arch intended to follow this sound advice his father had given to him many years ago.

9

Easter Sunday

Easter morning, Arch took advantage of the holiday and slept late. When he arose and looked about, he saw something that appeared to be new men's clothing in the form of a suit, shirt, tie and underclothes, along with a new pair of shoes and socks. Everything a man would need to dress up. He had no idea where these clothes came from, and an examination of them revealed they were his size, even the shoes. New shoes were something he hadn't seen since the Confederate army had invaded a little town in Pennsylvania just before the Battle of Gettysburg. Then he had failed to get a new pair because he couldn't find the right size.

He had always been told if the shoe fits then wear it, so after he had dressed in the new suit he tried on the new shoes and they fit, also. They were stiff, and would probably hurt his feet until they were broken in, but it was nice to be dressed up once again. It seemed that something was going on, but if it was this nice and pleasant he wouldn't complain. He felt sure he would find out what this meant before long.

About the time he completed dressing, his sister called and said, "When you have finished dressing, come into the kitchen. I have a surprise for you."

Now what kind of surprise could she have for him after what he had already been greeted with this morning? It must be something to do with these clothes. As he started to the kitchen he looked into the mirror. Looking back at him was a young man who, with a fresh haircut, would appear to be dressed to go sparking. Why hell, sparking was something he hadn't thought about in a long time. It brought back his memories of going sparking during the war with some of the pretty girls of Tennessee, but that had been a long time ago. Now maybe when he had time he should begin looking around for some lonesome lady who would like a little attention. He would have to think about this a little, but now he needed to find out what was going on in the kitchen.

He looked about as he entered the kitchen and when Sarah saw him she said, "I promised you a surprise and now you will get it." Walking to the door, she called out "You can come in now."

It was a surprise and a shock, for when he looked up he saw coming through the door his married sister, followed by a man who he assumed was her husband the preacher. When they embraced, both with tears of joy in their eyes, Arch said, "Oh God, it is so good to see you again! You will never know how many times I prayed the Lord would favor us by letting all of us come together again. Now my prayers have been answered and I thank Him."

Turning to the preacher he first stuck out his hand, but then instead of shaking hands they embraced. With tears now falling down their cheeks the room became very quiet. It was obvious that this meeting was not the first time these two men had met. The Preacher spoke first and in a quiet voice said, "You folks don't know this, but this man and I once met in another place in a different situation at another time. We don't want to discuss it now, but sometime in the future we will tell you about our first meeting. We didn't know each other's names then, but now here we are, together again. Let's enjoy this moment now and forget the past."

When the breakfast food had been prepared and they were all sitting around the table, the Preacher said grace, thanking Almighty God for the bountiful blessings he had bestowed upon them all. Then they filled their plates with the grits, eggs, ham and biscuit, a typical southern breakfast that they all enjoyed. When everyone had finished eating, hot coffee was served with fresh home-made cream and store-bought sugar.

Sitting around the table the adults enjoyed their coffee and talked. The boys went outside to play after being admonished not to get dirty as they were going to church later that morning. Everyone enjoyed the conversation and after a period the two men arose and went outside. They began to stroll about and naturally their conversation turned to their first meeting. The Preacher asked Arch if the wound he had received in his side ever gave him any trouble.

Arch answered, "No, I hardly know it is there, but I do feel the one I received earlier in my leg and it will probably bother me the rest of my life. It just don't feel right, but I suppose it's something I'll have to learn to live with."

The Preacher commented, "Well, you don't limp, so it will probably never give you any bad trouble other than the feeling being unnatural." He continued, "When I first saw you trying to minister and help those men in your company who had been wounded, I knew you were hurt worse than many of those you were helping, But I soon realized that you were determined to care for your men, even if it killed you to do so. That was why I insisted you let me look at your wound. Your biggest problem was the blood you were losing, and fortunately I was able to stop it."

"I appreciated what you did for me and the other men," replied Arch.

"That was a terrible battle, and I hope and pray I am never called upon to participate in anything that bad again. Old General Pickett thought he could stuff enough bodies into those cannon barrels to stop them from firing, but it just wasn't possible, was it?"

The Preacher thought for a few moments and then he responded by saying, "We did come mighty close to making that break through, but it just wasn't the will of the Almighty and we failed. I think that was the turning point in the war, don't you?"

"Yes," Arch replied.

"From that time on I was convinced that we couldn't win, but I would have walked through the front gates of Hell for General Lee, so I fought on until the end. I was at Appomattox when he surrendered. Were you there?"

"No," the Preacher said.

"I wish I could have been there, but I had been captured and was released soon after the armistice. I came on home and started making my rounds. Shortly after I returned, Mary and I were married. You know, I had courted her before I went into the army as a chaplain. We had already talked to your father and he approved. I am sorry he died before we married, but that was not the will of God."

Looking at his watch the Preacher said, "It's about time we started to church, isn't it?"

"Yes," replied Arch.

"I'll call the women and children and we can get started. It's such a beautiful morning I think we should walk. It will only take about a half-hour and everyone should enjoy it."

It was indeed a beautiful morning, and as they walked along the little road to the church, the wild flowers presented a lovely picture for all to appreciate. The delicate fragrance of the dogwood trees combined with the honeysuckles and other blooming flowers gave off a perfume that only God could have designed. Their beauty was a fitting memorial to commemorate the rising of the Lord Jesus Christ from the dead.

As they strolled along no one spoke, the only sound the rustling leaves in the trees as a gentle spring breeze stirred them. In the distance, the melody of the wild birds sounded as if they, too, were celebrating this joyous Easter Sunday. It was a very pleasant walk enjoyed by all, and when the church came into sight they were reluctant for the walk to end. The church was nestled beneath the large live oaks whose buds were turning green. Soon they would provide new foliage to shadow the earth during the coming months of summer. It was a wonderful time to enjoy and appreciate the beauty provided by a most benevolent God.

The church service consisted of the usual songs by the little congregation. The Preacher's sermon explained the rising of the Lord Jesus Christ and its importance to the basic foundation of the Christian religion. At the end of the service, after communion had been served to all who wished to participate, the altar was opened for those who wished to come and pray. After the first verse of the last song was sung, and the congregation began the last verse, Arch arose and walked slowly down the aisle. He knelt at the altar and bowed his head in prayer. He asked God to accept his humble appreciation for the love, protection and kindness he had provided him during his absence from church.

When he arose he noticed the Preacher had also come and knelt beside him and as their eyes met it was mutually understood that they both had offered a prayer of thanksgiving that morning. No words were necessary to confirm to each other that they both had known the awesome work of God on a personal level in days of the past.

Following the close of services, the congregation filed from the church, stopping to speak and howdy one another. After brief conversation, everyone seemed to fade from sight and Arch, accompanied by his family, retraced their steps home over the beautiful path they had walked earlier that morning.

Upon arriving home, the women changed their Sunday clothes and proceeded to the kitchen to begin preparing the noon meal. The men walked about talking about the crops Arch planned to begin planting and the condition of the animals. They enjoyed watching the two boys as they played.

This land was fertile and would provide an abundance of food in a great variety if one was persistent in their endeavor to grow and harvest it. Many fruits grew wild that would provide jellies, jams and preserves to be enjoyed during the long winter months ahead. Sarah had always been good at gathering these fruits and utilizing them in many ways which were appreciated by all.

Arch planned to plant several acres of corn, which when harvested, could be ground into grits and corn meal for the family. The surplus would be utilized to feed the work animals, the chickens and geese, and to fatten hogs that would be butchered for meat and lard. He would plant sweet potatoes that could be banked and eaten all year round. Sugar cane would be ground and the juice cooked into bright sweet syrup.

A small chufa patch would help fatten the hogs and required

little cultivation. Most of the food the family would require could be produced on the farm and any excess that was produced could be sold or traded at the store for those items they couldn't grow, such as wheat flour. Perhaps the surplus would even provide some cash money. They discussed Arch's plans and the Preacher offered several suggestions and advice.

The dinner was soon ready and they were called in to eat. This day had been one of the most enjoyable times Arch had spent since he had returned home. The food was delicious and everyone wished the meal could last forever, but that wasn't possible, as the Preacher and Mary would be leaving after the meal. Their journey back to their home would take a couple of days if they didn't encounter any difficulties, and then the Preacher would soon have to begin making his rounds to the churches in his circuit.

During the dinner, Arch's stepmother asked the Preacher if she and the two boys could accompany he and his wife when they returned home. She wished to go to her father's home to live and it wouldn't be out of the way as they would pass close by on the return trip home. She wasn't happy living in so isolated an area, and soon the boys would be old enough to go to school. Since this was the first time Arch had heard about this move, he thought it should be given some serious thought and consideration. But after the Preacher and both of his sisters expressed their support for the idea, he offered no objection.

Privately he told Sarah to give his stepmother five of the twenty dollar gold pieces she had hidden so his stepmother would have funds to pay her way and to support she and the boys after they arrived at her father's home.

After his stepmother had packed their meager belongings, they were placed in the Preacher's wagon and the little group departed. It was going to be a thrilling experience for the boys who had never been farther from home than the church. They were so excited they couldn't wait to leave, and when they were ready to go, they each came to Arch. They hugged his neck and told him he would have to come and visit them at their grandfather's home.

Later, after they departed, Arch felt quite depressed and lonesome. He wandered about, seeking something he could become interested in to help forget the loneliness that now prevailed. He had grown attached to the little fellows, and now they were gone.

10

The Crops

In the days that followed Easter, Arch worked very diligently to accomplish a multitude of tasks he had laid out for himself before he began to plant. This constant work helped him to fill the void created by the absence of the two little half-brothers he had become quite fond of and now missed so badly. Many times he would work at jobs that should have been accomplished by several men, but his determination soon resulted in the completion of these difficult tasks. When he looked back on them, he realized they hadn't been as difficult as he had imagined they would be. This gave him a feeling of accomplishment and the loneliness that had existed soon passed and was forgotten.

Each morning, seven days a week, he would leave the house before dawn watching the sun rise as he began the work he planned for that day. He would return home after dark completely exhausted. Sarah would perform the many chores around the house that he would normally handle, relieving him from the responsibility. She would have his meals cooked, ready for him to eat when he returned after each long day working in the fields.

Once the fields were tilled and the crops had been planted, the task of cultivating began. The weeds and other growth began to outgrow his crops. To destroy them Arch had to plow each row, and in some cases it was necessary to hoe the vegetation that couldn't be destroyed by plowing with the mule. The hoeing required many hours of back-breaking hard work, but soon he had accomplished this task and his crops began to flourish.

Maintaining the house, cooking their meals, and performing the many chores that Arch normally performed kept Sarah very busy, and left little time for she and Arch to discuss the events each had faced that day. Arch was tired from his long hours of work in the fields, and each night after going to the creek for bathing, he would eat his supper, excuse himself, and soon be in bed sound asleep. Exhaustion from the long hours of hard work left both with little time for themselves, but Arch promised Sarah that when the crops had been laid by, they would then rest and enjoy themselves.

One day, he returned home early because of a thunderstorm, and noticed that Sarah had started to paint again, something she had learned when she attended school in Savannah. Her pictures of wild flowers and scenes of the surrounding woodlands were very beautiful, and portrayed a realistic vision of the scenery along the creeks and river. These settings provided ample inspiration for her to observe and paint. The realism of her river scenes fascinated him, and made him wish to build a boat that would allow them to drift down the river with the tides, providing her many more pretty scenes to paint while he fished.

This would have to wait until he had finished laying the crops by. If everything went as planned, when summer arrived he would withdraw from the fields and then they could enjoy some moments of leisure. He thought that if he worked doubly hard, he could finish working the fields by the latter part of June. This would be a good time for him to fish and the plants and trees along the river banks would be at their height of beauty, providing Sarah the opportunity to record these wonderful sights through her paintings.

He longed to sit in the shade of a big tree alongside the riverbank, where he could drop a big earthworm down in an eddy spot in the bend of the river. His imagination would form a picture of a big blue gill bream sucking the worm down, and when the cork began to bobble, the bream would run the length of his line, sinking the cork completely from sight. He envisioned the following struggle would cause his heart to beat faster and he could imagine how he would feel when he had finally landed this prize. His vision continued with he and his sister sitting at the table with a plate full of fried bream, corn dodgers filled with chopped onions all fried to a golden brown perfection, topped off with a cup of hot coffee. He could hardly wait for these visions to become a reality.

He knew that before he could indulge in any fishing he would have to finish all the cultivation of his crops, so he began to work every waking hour in an effort to finish on time.

In the latter part of June, the hot weather became unbearable. As he was leaving home one morning to hoe corn, he told Sarah that if it didn't rain that day, and nothing unusual happened, he would be finished that afternoon before he returned home.

Arch hadn't told Sarah that he had found an abandoned boat floating down the river one day. After swimming out into the river to retrieve it, he secured it to a tree in a little cove near the field he had been working. It wasn't much of a boat, but it would carry them about, and until someone appeared to claim it, they would use it. In his spare time, during the extremely hot part of the day, he had made some repairs to the boat and now it no longer leaked and appeared to be stable.

When he arrived home late that afternoon with the news that he had finished hoeing the corn, he told Sarah he had grunted worms for them to go fishing the next morning. Her excitement was obvious and when morning arrived she was prepared for a day on the river.

11

The Fishing Trip

Early the next morning after finishing the fine breakfast Sarah had prepared for him, Arch went into the lot yard, and using a potato rake, began to dig about where the animals fed. Soon he began to find large white grubs which could be used for bait along with the earthworms he had grunted the previous afternoon. When Arch was confident he had enough bait he called Sarah and announced that it was time for them to begin their fishing trip. The previous afternoon he had cut and rigged two reeds to be used for the bream fishing.

Arriving at the water's edge, he placed the bait and poles into the boat, and Sarah added food and water for them to enjoy while they fished. She had brought her pad and pencils to sketch the different scenes that would be seen along the riverbank whenever she tired of fishing.

Arch sculled the boat out into the current of the river, where it drifted slowly along until they arrived at a sharp bend. Here Arch tied the boat to a limb that extended from the shore. He baited Sarah's pole with a long earthworm since she didn't like to handle the worms, and they began to fish in an eddy spot. The long earthworms proved to be the better bait, and soon Sarah's cork went down. When she pulled the pole it began to bend, which meant something big had taken her bait.

After struggling for several minutes, she brought to the surface a large catfish. Arch quickly landed the catfish in the boat and removed the sharp fins that protruded from each side of the fish's head and back. These fins were dangerous, but now that they had been removed, they no longer presented any problem and the fish was tied to a long string that was secured to the boat. The fish could now be returned to the water and remain alive.

As the morning passed they continued to catch fish, and by noon they had caught a variety of different species, including blue gill bream, red bellies, stump knockers, bass, warmouth, and the big catfish Sarah had caught earlier. When they tired of fishing, they realized there were more fish on the stringer than they could consume in several meals, so Arch decided he would take the surplus to town and attempt to exchange them with the storekeeper for some items they couldn't raise on the farm.

When Sarah tired of fishing she took her pad and began sketching the different flowers that grew along the river bank. The rough drafts of these plants and the scenes she outlined would provide her with enough material to occupy her spare time for many days. Arch asked to see the pictures when she had completed them. He knew it would be a while before she would have time to finish them.

Soon Arch tired of fishing. He untied the boat and began to scull back up the river to the cove that had been their point of departure earlier that morning. The tide had changed while they were fishing and now the river was running stronger in the opposite direction. He realized that the tide would only get stronger until it reached the low point and began to rise. They would have to wait because he couldn't scull against the falling water.

When they were finally able to return to the cove he tied the boat up, realizing that they had spent almost the entire day on their excursion. He wouldn't have time to go to town with the excess fish, so he decided to clean them and salt them down, preserving them until they could be eaten later.

That night he and Sarah feasted on the fresh fish with fried Irish potatoes, and hush puppies made from corn meal, store-bought flour, and seasoned with chipped onions and other condiments. They also enjoyed pickled peaches and cucumbers, a meal even better than he had dreamed of many months before. It was truly a delightful evening.

After they had finished their supper, they carried two chairs out into the yard and sat enjoying the bright stars that illuminated the heavens and the surrounding area of their home. Soon the largest full moon either could remember began to rise above the treetops, and they became engrossed in the beauty of it all. It was a wonderful sight, as if the Lord had designed this beauty for only them to observe and enjoy. When they began to become sleepy, they arose and went into the house, each going to their bed to dream of the wonderful day they had experienced.

Arch fell asleep quickly and dreamed of fishing the river and enjoying the surroundings. It had been such a long time since he had been able to relax, but suddenly a noise awoke him. Lying in his bed, listening intently, he heard the noise again, more clearly this time. Realizing that someone was outside, he quietly rose from his bed. He quickly slipped on his pants, removed his rifle from the rack on the wall, and began to creep to the door. Suddenly he heard Sarah whisper, "Did you hear it too?" Without speaking, he motioned for her to get her pistol. As she watched, he carefully and quietly eased out the door into the dark night. He was a soldier once again, his mind on the sound which had disturbed his sleep. His senses were alert to any movement that might reveal the whereabouts of the person who had invaded his home. The question was for what purpose, and this was something he intended to find out.

When he had been outside a few moments, his eyes became adjusted to the dark and he observed a man near the lot yard with what appeared to be a sack. He was filling it with meat that he had taken from the smokehouse.

Arch's first instinct had been to shoot the man, but instead he decided to watch and observe his movements. As he watched, the man returned to the smokehouse, leaving the sack of meat. Arch could see the man beginning to cut down more meat. While his attention was diverted, Arch slipped up to the sack of meat that had been left outside. He picked it up and moved it several steps from where the man had left it. With his arms loaded with hams and shoulders, the man, who Arch now realized was black, emerged from the smokehouse. Going to the spot where he had left the sack of meat, he looked about frantically, puzzled when he couldn't locate the sack. It was obvious the man knew that someone was watching his every move, and when he saw the barrel of Arch's gun pointed at him, he dropped everything. He ran to a nearby tree and tried to hide behind it.

Since the man offered no danger to either he or his sister, Arch decided to let him go. He would track him down tomorrow. Returning to the house he found Sarah standing just inside the door with her double barrel pistol cocked, ready to fire if necessary. As he entered the house he told her, "I don't think our visitor will return tonight, so we might as well go back to bed. I'll re-hang the meat in the morning before I track down the would-be thief."

Sarah didn't like a thief any better than her brother, but she dreaded to think what Arch might do to the man when he caught him. She had little doubt he would track him down, and she imagined his actions would be severe. She hoped he wouldn't kill the man.

The next morning, while Sarah prepared their breakfast, Arch re-hung the meat in the smokehouse. The intruder didn't know that this additional work only fueled Arch's determination to catch him. When he had finished this job he returned to the house. After washing up, he sat down at the table and waited for his sister to finish cooking their meal. As he sat there, pondering his next move, he soon realized it might take some time to catch his thief. No matter. Whatever time it required, he was determined to catch that man and put a stop to his stealing. There wasn't much conversation during breakfast and when he finished eating, Arch arose and announced, "The time has come for me to do a little tracking and find out who our visitor was last night."

Going to the gun rack, Arch removed his Yankee rifle, and after placing several cartridges in his pocket, he left the room and was soon out of sight. Sarah only hoped everything would turn out all right knowing that Arch wouldn't stop until he had discovered the identity of the thief.

Many years earlier in his youth, Arch had been taught to track by the old Indian. Now he would see if he had learned his lessons well. He followed the running tracks through the woods and soon arrived at the river. He could see where a boat had been dragged up on the bank the night before. Now he had a problem, since the river didn't leave any tracks to follow.

Sitting down on a log to think the situation over, he decided to take his boat out. While the tide in the river was falling, he would drift down river until the tide changed. He could watch the riverbank for signs where the intruder had left the river. If he found nothing when the tide began to rise, he would scull back to his landing and try again the next morning. He would go upstream until the water began to fall. He believed that the intruder had probably gone ashore within the distance he could go on one tide. Perhaps he would find the man's boat and then he wouldn't be too far from the culprit.

As he drifted along the river, his thoughts turned to the beauty of the plants and trees along the river's edge. He never tired of these sights and he particularly appreciated the beautiful wild roses that adorned the shore and the colorful flowers that made an elaborate pastel panorama. He observed snakes lounging on logs and vines, patiently waiting for an unexpected victim to come close enough to permit its capture and become the snake's meal of the day. Large alligators were sunning themselves on the logs which lay in the river and at its' edge, but each time he came close they would slip noiselessly into the water. They would eventually come back to the surface, allowing only their eyes and the end of their nose to protrude out of the water. Several disappeared and were not seen again until he returned on his way back to the landing. They would resume their position, lying on their log enjoying the sun's heat until he reappeared and disturbed them again.

The water became still as the wind became calm and he realized his trip down river was fast coming to an end. When the river reversed its' course he began to scull along toward the landing. He had enjoyed his uneventful morning, but he hadn't learned anything that would help him in his quest to find out who his uninvited visitor had been. The sights he had observed had made the trip enjoyable and he decided that his next trip would include a fishing pole and some bait so he could fish while he drifted along.

It was late when he returned home and he was very happy when he discovered all the chores had already been taken care of by Sarah, and his supper was cooked and ready for him to eat. While he ate he told Sarah of his trip and described the sights and the colorful flowers he had seen. He suggested she go with him the next day when he went upriver, but she declined, saying that she wasn't feeling too well and would rather go some other time. In reality, she didn't want to be there if he should happen to locate their uninvited guest, as she was apprehensive about what might happen.

As darkness closed in, the whippoorwills began their nightly calls, seeking their companions, and the occasional hoot owl would notify the world that he was awake and prowling the countryside for his supper and the companionship of his mate. After listening for a little while, Arch and Sarah became sleepy and retired for the night.

12

The Trip Upstream

By leaving early the next morning, Arch was able to take advantage of the rising tide, and going upstream was easy, requiring little effort. He brought along his fishing pole and a can of worms and as the boat drifted along he enjoyed some fishing. The warm morning sun made him drowsy. If he hadn't been interrupted by fish biting in unusually larger numbers, he would have gone to sleep. He was surprised that he caught so many fish. Alligator sightings, snakes, and the sight of the glorious flowers helped keep him awake.

He saw several old hen wood ducks with their broods of little ducklings, something he hadn't seen since he was a small boy. Each time he would encounter these hens they would flap along the water as if they were crippled, attempting to convince him they could be easily caught when in reality they were trying to divert his attention from the little ducklings. This gave the babies time to scamper away and hide in the brush along the riverside. After he would pass, the old hens would return to their original locations to re-gather their broods. It was amazing to watch these wild birds simulate this strategy in an effort to protect their young from this invader of their territory.

When he had about convinced himself that he wouldn't have any better luck this morning than he had the previous morning, he drifted around a bend in the river. There, on the right, was a lake making off from the river. Looking through the trees that sheltered the cove, he could see people sitting near a fire and a beached boat. To avoid being seen, he proceeded quickly to the riverbank and secured his boat. He could see a black man, and woman and several children squatting around the fire. They didn't see him until he spoke, saying "Good morning."

They were startled and jumped to their feet when they saw him. The sight of Arch with his rifle under his arm made them afraid. As he approached, the black man turned toward him and said, "I knew you would come, but before you shoot me please, master, let me explain. I know I was wrong to attempt to steal your meat and I should have tried to work out a trade, but I was desperate. My children and my wife were starving and I needed some food for them so badly."

He continued, "You see, we were promised freedom by Mr. Lincoln, but he didn't tell us that when we left the plantation we would have to provide for ourselves. We were just dumb Negroes who left and come down the river. We didn't give any thought to how we would survive. I did think I could fish, and kill an occasional alligator to sell the hide for cash money. It just didn't work out that way and my family is about to starve to death. I am ready to take my punishment for trying to steal your meat, but I hope and pray you will remember my wife and children depend on me to live."

Later, Arch told Sarah he couldn't help but feel sorry for the man and after listening to him and observing his pitiful condition he had responded by telling him, "You know you were wrong to attempt to steal my meat, but I am going to offer you an opportunity to earn that meat, and if you will work hard, we might make a deal that will allow you the chance to provide shelter and food for your family in the future without stealing it."

"I have a farm and need help to operate it," continued Arch.

"If you are sincere, you be at my house this afternoon before sundown and I'll give you your first installment of food."

Arch then returned to his boat. As he untied it, he called to the man, "Come down here to my boat and I'll give you some fish I caught this morning. I think there is enough to feed your family today." After they had been given the fish, Arch sculled the boat back out into the river and began to drift downstream on the now falling tide.

Drifting down the river toward home, Arch gave much thought to the decision he had made that morning. Why he hadn't taken more drastic action he really didn't know, but perhaps giving this poor destitute man and his starving family a chance might be one of the best decisions he had ever made. It hadn't cost him anything and the little food he now planned to give wouldn't make a significant impact on his life in the future. There was plenty more meat in the woods and with his knowledge of hunting it wouldn't take long to replace all he had decided to give this family. He needed help to expand the farm, and if he offered this man the opportunity to farm the lower field, during the summer he could clear up more land. Then he could offer him a portion of the crops they would grow on the newly cleared fields. Such a situation would call for trust on both sides, and Arch would be required to advance enough food to carry the man and his family over until the crops could be grown and harvested. He remembered those days during his long journey home from the war when he had been hungry and this made the decision easier to reach. He would build them a small house near his home so that he could learn more about the man and his family.

Sarah was surprised when she saw a black man and two boys approaching the house, but any anxiety she had was quickly dispelled when the man knocked on the door humbly with his hat in his hand. She could see this man needed help, and when he explained that her brother, referring to Arch as "the man with the gun," had told him to come to the farm before sundown, she knew this was the uninvited visitor. She said a silent prayer, thanking God that Arch hadn't taken the drastic action she had been afraid he might take when he found this man.

She explained that her brother hadn't returned and they would have to wait until he arrived. The man asked, "Would it be alright if we got a drink of water?"

Sarah answered, "Yes, you may have all the water you want. I think I have some pone that your boys might enjoy with some of my pear preserves." Disappearing into the house she soon returned and handed each of the boys and the man a large slice of corn pone. Pears could be seen protruding between the slices.

She saw the sheer delight on their faces, and after they had eaten their food, they went to the well and drew a bucket of water. They each took a long drink from the gourd dipper that hung from a nail on the post near the well.

Soon they could see Arch coming from the direction of the river. When he arrived, he and Sarah went into the house. After discussing with Sarah what he intended to do, Arch came back outside. Going to the smokehouse, he began to collect the food he had promised the man. He told the man that his would feed his family until he could move them to the farm. When he had gathered all the food, he turned to the man and asked, "What is your name? Please tell me because I don't intend to call you "Boy" like I imagine you were called on the plantation you came from."

Smiling, the man replied, "Boss, I have always been called John, but I don't have a last name like the white master I belonged to before the President made us free."

"Well John, I think that will be adequate until we find a last name for you," said Arch.

"Now take this food back to your family and tomorrow you make plans to move them to my farm. You can live in the barn until we can build your family a house. The barn will be a better place than that hut your entire family is living in now. Why, if you tried to live there this winter, I imagine you all would die from exposure. It will take some time to cut logs and drag them to that spot over there by the big red oak on the other side of the house."

Pointing to the spot he was referring to Arch continued, saying, "Now, you better get started before it gets dark. And by the way, you might take the old mule and the two wheel cart to move your belongings in tomorrow."

He could see from the expression on John's face that he was surprised, not expecting such an offer. As John began to bow he removed his hat and expressed his gratitude by saying, "Boss, I didn't expect anything like this, but are you sure you want to trust me with your mule and cart?"

Arch smiled, and looked down at the ground to hide his amusement at the response he had received. After several seconds he looked up and replied, "I think I can trust you, but if I find my trust has been misplaced, you know I'll find you."

"Yes sir, I know you would," John replied.

John and his two sons went into the lot yard, caught the mule, harnessed and hitched him to the cart, and began to load the food they had been given. It consisted of smoked pork, venison, corn meal, grits, syrup, sweet potatoes, and a small bag of coffee beans.

Arch explained as they were loading the cart with the supplies he had given them that when the family had been moved to the farm, they would be given an allotment of food each week for the work they performed. He emphasized, "no work" meant "no food", so they were aware that he expected them to work and earn the food. When working on the farm raising crops, Arch and Sarah would feed them. Any surplus that would be sold would be divided, enabling them to purchase at the store those things they required that couldn't be produced on the farm.

His fairness impressed John and that night he told his family what they could expect. While his wife was apprehensive, remembering the treatment they had received from the white people that had owned them on the plantation, John's assurance that this white man was different and could be trusted helped her to make the decision to move to Arch's farm the next day.

John and his family returned to the farm with their few belongings piled on the cart much earlier than Arch had anticipated. After they arrived, Arch had them move the farm equipment that had been stored in the barn, and now there was adequate space for them to live until a house could be built. This provided a much better place for them than the little hut where they had been existing.

Arch told John, "To build a house that will be solid and tight will take a lot of hard work and time. You people will have to all begin work now if this is to come about."

John said, "Boss, me and my boys will do anything you tell us to do. We can help you build the house and the sooner the better."

The following morning, while the family busied themselves getting their living quarters in the barn arranged, Arch went into the woods and selected several large yellow pines that stood not too far from the barn. After he decided where the house would be placed, he returned and told John and the two largest boys to be ready the next morning to go into the woods to begin cutting the trees he had selected. These large yellow pines would provide the walls of the house. After they had been moved to the site of the house, they would be squared and notched before being placed in the walls using an "A" frame and his block and tackle. The mule would provide the power to lift the logs into place. When they had been moved to the correct location, Arch planned to have the boys drill holes down each corner and a fat lightered pole would be inserted to hold them in a stable position. Later, the cracks would be chinked with clay and pine straw to prevent the cold wind from entering during the winter and provide a warm wall inside.

He instructed the boys to sharpen the axes and to oil the crosscut saw they would use to fell the large trees. He explained that they would be required to work long hours to ensure that the house would be livable before the corn crop matured and was ready to be broken. The fodder would be ready in just a few weeks and the space they were now occupying in the barn would be needed to store these crops.

Arch knew he would have to establish a new schedule that would allow for the building of a house. He understood there would be problems that he had not anticipated earlier and they would have to keep working long hours to prevent the loss of his badly needed crops, especially now, since he had six more mouths to feed.

During the weeks that followed, the work on the house progressed slowly. Finally, the logs were cut and the boys began to drag them to the spot where the house would be built while

Arch and John prepared the site. When the task of moving the logs had been completed, Arch began to instruct John and the boys how to measure each log. After the logs had been cut into the correct length, they would notch them to permit them to fit snugly together when assembled in the wall. To raise each log and place them in the position they would occupy in the wall, they had to build an "A" frame. Utilizing the old block and tackle that he and his father had used many years before when the house Arch now lived in was constructed, they soon had walls in place. They used the mule to pull the rope as each log was raised and placed in the wall.

When the outside walls were about seven feet high, the doors and windows were cut and then a final log was placed around the entire structure. Each corner was secured with an iron rod inserted through the entire height of the wall. This would hold the logs in place and prevent any movement that would displace the walls. These iron rods were also inserted in the walls where each door and window had been cut.

There would be a dirt floor and the roof would be made from the cypress shingles split from the blocks they cut from dried cypress logs found along the riverbank. After nailing strips of pine pole to serve as lathing on the pine rafters, the roof was soon completed. The work had been slow to Arch. He was eager to complete the job before it became time to harvest his crops, which were maturing fast.

Each phase of the construction was slow, mainly because of the inexperience of John and the boys, but it gradually evolved into a livable house. True, the cracks between the log walls remained to be chinked with clay and pine straw, and the outside doors had to be built. But they could move in and complete the remainder of the work after the matured crops had been gathered and stored in the space in the barn they would no longer need to occupy. The corn would soon be broken and stored in the barn, along with the fodder they would place in the attic of the barn.

Now the squirrels and other rodents would not destroy the fruit of Arch's labor. They would grind the corn into meal and grits after it had been shelled and placed in barrels to prevent the weevils from infiltrating it and making it unusable for food. Arch's father taught him to place small containers of formaldehyde in each barrel to repel these insects and prevent them from destroying the corn.

13

Harvest Time

Pulling the fodder from the corn stalks was a nasty job. Dust from the shucks would fall into the person's clothing and cause a very irritating itch. To avoid this, the puller would tie their shirt sleeves, button their collar and keep their clothes tightly wound around their bodies, but still the dust would penetrate. The day the fodder pulling was completed was a day to celebrate, and enjoy the fact that it would be another year before this task would be required again.

Breaking the corn was a job to be done when it was dry and before the varmints could destroy it. The workers would break several rows each round through the field, and make piles would be made between the corn rows being broken. The two boys would drive the mule pulling the two-wheel cart down the rows where the corn had been piled. When the body of the cart was full they would take the load to the barn and unload it. It would be kept there until it was needed to feed the animals. Soon the part of the barn that had been allocated for corn was full. Each succeeding load was then placed on top of the pile until the joists overhead were touching the corn. This year there was a most bountiful crop and Arch could look at the now harvested corn and feel thankful and quite proud of the results of his hard work.

The next task was to dig the sweet potatoes and build a sweet potato bank. This was done by digging a large hole, lining it with pine straw and then placing the sweet potatoes in the circular hole. They would be covered with a layer of pine straw and a pyramid or tee pee structure was made above the hole by placing boards or corn stalks to form a peak. The entire structure would then be covered with several inches of dirt to prevent the potatoes from being frostbitten when the weather became cold and the ground froze. An opening was made on the south side of the potato bank. This way when dirt was removed, access could be made to retrieve the potatoes when needed.

Arch's trap pens had worked much better than he had anticipated and he soon had twelve big barrows to fatten and butcher. They were placed in a large pen constructed from pine poles arranged to form a square. He placed two large wooden troughs inside, and Arch assigned John's boys the task of keeping the troughs full, one of corn and food scraps and the other filled with water. Long ago he had been told by his father to include oak ashes in the diet of fattening hogs. This would cause the corn to soften and rid the hogs of worms. His father said the potash from the ashes would kill any worms in the hogs and allow them to fatten quicker. As the hogs grew bigger and fatter it became necessary to increase the amount of feed the hogs were fed. He planned to have a hog killing when the weather turned extremely cold. These twelve barrows would provide meat and lard during the winter and spring along with the hogs he thought he might catch in the trap pens during the winter months. Hopefully this would be all the meat they needed until time came the next year to have another hog killing.

They still had one big job remaining, and that was the harvesting the sugar cane. First it had to be stripped, removing the dead leaves that were attached to each stalk. Then they would cut each stalk near the ground and place the stalks in a pile. They would then cover the stalks with the dead leaves to prevent the cane from frostbite until it was moved to the sugar mill.

Once at the mill, it would be fed in between the rollers to be crushed, allowing the sweet juice to be removed. The sugar mill was powered by the mule. He would prod around the mill, pulling a long pole that was attached to the top of the mill. This turned the rollers that powered the mill. After the juice had been extracted it was placed into a large kettle. It would then be boiled until all the water had evaporated and only the sweet, bright syrup remained. As the juice was cooked, a scum would form on top of the boiling juice. This scum would be removed and placed in a barrel known as the "buck barrel." Cooking the juice into syrup required large amounts of dried wood to fire the furnace. Arch decided that he and John would cut the wood and haul it to the furnace while the two boys stripped and cut the cane.

When everything had been hauled to the sugar mill, it was time to make the syrup. The sugar kettle held one hundred gallons of juice and was placed on four iron posts about two feet above the ground. It was enclosed with lime rock and mortared together with clay. One side had a door through which wood could be inserted to fire the kettle. Near the furnace door stood the smokestack. A wall extended from the smokestack to the center of the underside of the kettle permitted the fire to be built near the door. The draft would draw the fire around the bottom of the kettle providing an even fire over the entire bottom. Arch watched his father build the sugar furnace and knew exactly how it worked.

One cool morning when everything had been cut and hauled to the sugar furnace, they began the process of making syrup. The mule was hitched to the cane mill and began his steady prodding around the mill. This pulled the wheels together, and they crushed the cane that the boys were inserting between the rollers. As the juice flowed into the barrel it was removed and placed into the kettle until it was filled. The fire was then started and soon the juice began to boil. Arch carefully removed the scum as the juice cooked, and placed it in the buck barrel. It remained there until the fermentation process was complete.

It then could be distilled into liquor commonly known as "cane buck" and some called it "moonshine." It wasn't the best liquor, but it was better than nothing if someone wanted a drink. There was one drawback to drinking this liquor besides the headache that often followed its consumption. This was the large number of bees it attracted, which would swarm around anyone partaking of this ambrosia. The bees would fly around the drinker's face and become a nuisance. Sometimes this resulted in the person being stung when they would attempt to brush the bees away. Bee stings were quite painful and most individuals would rather avoid the bees by not partaking of the drink.

The "cane buck" could be consumed without being run through a still, but again there was a drawback. If the fermentation process hadn't completed its cycle, it would have a very undesirable effect on one's stomach. Another use for the "buck" was to feed it to the fattening hogs. If provided to the hogs in large quantities they would become drunk and lay around as if they were dead until they sobered up. Then they would seek more of the buck, acting very much like an alcoholic. Arch preferred to have happy hogs in his fattening pen so he would insist that the boys feed the buck to the hogs.

After several days of cooking syrup the process was finished. Now there was a supply of syrup that would last through the year. A small amount would be carried to the store and traded for items they couldn't grow on the farm. It was wonderful to have a surplus that might provide a small amount of cash money.

Now that all the major tasks had been completed ,time passed with only the hog killing left to be done when the weather became cold enough. Some days would be cold and then a warm period would follow, which postponed the killing of the hogs. Finally a long period of cold arrived and the hogs were killed and placed in the smokehouse to be cured and smoked.

Arch decided it was time for him to begin hunting. He worked at this as if he were going to the field each morning and would spend long days seeking the elusive deer and wild hogs that roamed the swamp. With John and the boys to handle the chores, he would arise before daylight each morning and go into the woods before dawn. Some days his luck would be poor; occasionally he would return bearing the fruits of his labor. The deer he killed would be skinned and placed in the smokehouse to be salted and cured, much as the pork would be preserved. Several times he was lucky and killed fat hogs which he also placed in the smokehouse. When he killed a turkey either his sister or John's wife would cook it and they would have a feast on the unfortunate bird.

Life was good and they enjoyed this time of year. At night they sat around a fire with their families remembering the days long past and dreaming of the pleasant times the future would bring. Since it was unseasonably warm that year, they celebrated Christmas by having a dinner out under the trees. They held a special Christmas service as if they were in the church. Sarah read the Christmas story of the birth of Christ and they sang seasonal songs. It was something everyone enjoyed. Christmas dinner, with its special dishes of food, brought the realization that while they were not wealthy, they were rich in many material things and should be thankful for the many blessings that God had bestowed on them.

John said, "Boss, you and Miss Sarah have been the kindest people us Negroes have ever known. You treat us as if we were kin and I hope that we never cause you to think of us any other way. My wife and all our children love you both and thank you for the kind treatment you have shown us."

Both Arch and Sarah were touched and found it difficult to know what to say in response. Finally Arch said, "Well, you all know we have very kind feelings for your entire family. Since you came we have accomplished much and I feel certain that the future will hold many wonderful things for all of us."

After they had sat about and talked away the afternoon it became time to attend to the chores. Everyone returned home to begin the work that had to be done even though it was Christmas Day.

14

The New Cycle

Following the holidays of Christmas and New Years they began to clear more land, providing new fields to plant. This was hard, backbreaking work that began early each morning and ended late in the afternoon. They would return home just early enough to perform the chores, feed the animals and eat their supper before bedtime. Cutting the smaller trees, digging the stumps and girding the larger trees left them extremely tired at the end of each day, but the cleared areas grew larger and larger. Now they could grow larger crops and produce greater volumes of produce, and surpluses could be sold or bartered for other things they would need. This knowledge stimulated their desire to work harder each day in order to achieve their goals.

Once while Arch was in town purchasing supplies he was

approached by a man who exhibited a keen interest in the Negroes who he had been told worked and resided on Arch's farm. He stated that these Negroes had been slaves on a plantation in Georgia where he worked as the supervisor for the plantation owner. He asked Arch questions about John and his family and suggested that they should return to the plantation and work for him.

"I have difficulties finding workers since the Negroes were emancipated and I am trying To find those slaves who used to work on the plantation before Lincoln set them free," said the man.

"I can make them return, and they will be sorry if they don't."

After listening to what the man had to say, Arch replied, "Mister, I fought the North for six years of my life and we lost. The President of the United States issued a proclamation that freed these people from slavery and gave them the right to live and work where they choose. John and his family chose my farm to live on and work, and I see no wrong with their decision. If you and your plantation owner attempt to force their return against their wishes, I'll put you on notice now there will be more trouble than you can imagine."

Turning to leave, the man said, "You might think you can steal my Negroes, but you will find we don't take kindly to people who cross us."

"Are you threatening me, fellow?" asked Arch.

"Because if you are, we can settle this right now and you won't be going back to Georgia."

The man, who had a pistol strapped around his waist, turned back. After seeing the Sharps rifle in Arch's hand, he again turned away and walked across the street to the saloon without making any further comment.

The old black storekeeper had heard the exchange and waited until Arch was inside and out of the hearing of the other man.

"I don't want you to think I am trying to tend to your business," said the storekeeper, "but you had better be careful where that man and his boss are concerned. From what I hear, they will go to any length to return all their former slaves to their plantation."

Arch smiled and replied, "I appreciate your concern, and thank you. By the way, don't you sell guns?"

"What type of gun are you interested in?" asked the storekeeper.

I'm interested in a pistol because at times it's difficult to carry this rifle," said Arch. "Sometimes I need to have my hands free. I'm also interested in the little Remington roll block twenty-two rifles, like those up on the wall."

The storekeeper left the room and went into another room at the back of the store building. He soon returned with several pistols which showed considerable wear from use; however, one of them, a .41 caliber revolver that was designed to fire a brass cartridge instead of the cap and ball system of the others. It looked extremely good. When Arch questioned him about this weapon the storekeeper told him it would cost more than the others, especially if he wanted the matching holster.

"This is a good pistol," remarked the storekeeper.

"It shoots very accurately, and I know this because I have fired it several times myself. Now, I could sell you one of these old Walkers for about six dollars, but this one with the holster will cost twelve dollars, including a box of ammunition. I think you will find it worth the difference."

Arch studied the pistol more closely, hefting it in his hand and sighting down the barrel. After his examination, he reached into his pocked and extracted two ten dollar gold pieces.

"I'll give you this amount for the pistol, the holster, and a box of bullets," said Arch.

"You'll also need to throw in two of those little single shot twenty-two rifles and two boxes of cartridges for them."

The storekeeper pondered the offer for a few moments and finally said, "You got a deal." He wrapped the other items Arch had purchased, giving a questioning look as he picked up the two rifles. Arch said, "Just wrap them in a burlap bag that I can tie behind my saddle and I'll take care of the pistol and the holster myself."

Arch picked up the pistol and holster and strapped the holster around his waist. He then opened the cylinder of the pistol and inserted six cartridges into it before placing it in the holster.

As he rode home he felt more secure even though he had always had his Sharps and was confident that with it he could match most anyone with a gun. Now he wouldn't have to borrow Sarah's double barrel pistol when he went to town.

His intentions were to give each on of John's two boys the twenty-two rifles that he would use to teach them shooting skills. They could hunt small game when they were not busy and it would give them a sense of security when they were in the woods. You never could tell when you might come across a rattlesnake or a bad wild hog, and now when they encountered these varmints they could protect themselves.

It was almost dark when Arch arrived home. As he rode past John's house he called the boys and told them, "I have a surprise for you, but you will have to wait until morning to receive it. Come to the house in the morning about sunrise and I'll give the surprise to you." He thought perhaps it was a little cruel to tell them this, for now their curiosity would probably keep them awake tonight wondering what the surprise could be.

Bright and early the next morning, just as the sun began to peep through the trees, the two boys arrived in front of Arch's house. When he unwrapped the two twenty-two rifles he had never seen two more excited boys. After he gave each boy their new rifle with basic instruction on how the bolt and safety worked, he led them into the woods. He placed a target on a tree and allowed each to take a shot at it. He was surprised how well they listened to his sighting instructions and how quickly they hit the target since they had never had access to a gun before. He cautioned them to use the guns carefully and admonished them, saying "Should I see you using the guns carelessly or in a manner that is dangerous, I'll take them back." They each assured him he didn't have anything to worry about, and promised that they would take good care of the guns and use them exactly as he had instructed them.

When they returned home, Arch showed the boys how to care for their guns to keep them in good working order.

15

Time Passes By

Days turned into weeks and weeks into months and months became years and their lives went on. Everything in the life of these people proceeded in an orderly manner. Sometimes they would encounter problems, but even during these times they enjoyed their lives.

The crops were bountiful, providing them with an abundance of food and other materials that they could sell or barter away. The stock multiplied and the herds expanded, requiring larger areas to provide the browse necessary for them to grow. Work became a routine, and John's two largest boys matured into fine young men, now capable of assuming responsibilities and assisting their father and Arch in all the facets of the farm's operation.

Soon Arch assigned each boy the responsibility of one of the fields, and although they were permitted to make their own decisions, both Arch and John maintained a watchful eye over the work they were performing, offering advice when something appeared questionable.

Arch purchased two new mules and a horse. This provided John and each of the boys with a mule to plow, and the horse served as a mode of transportation. They rode the woods, keeping a close watch over the ever-growing herds of cattle and hogs. While the hogs didn't wander as far away as the cattle, Arch was constantly required to expand the range he oversaw in order to maintain an awareness of the cattle location. This required more of his time and soon became a full time job. It was, however, necessary to prevent someone from laying claim to the cattle that bore the big "M" brand with the marked ears of crop right and a swallow fork left.

Almost everyone in the countryside knew who the owner of these cattle and hogs was, and most respected the integrity of their owner's identity. Seldom would anyone bother these animals. They knew the owner was a man who constantly watched over his herds and the ever-present Sharps rifle could be seen on his saddle. They knew he wouldn't hesitate to use the gun if he caught one of them molesting or stealing any of his animals.

Arch made a practice of never selling any of his cattle or hogs bearing his mark and brand, thereby eliminating any doubt that the animals bearing these identifying marks belonged to him.

Each fall he would round up two and three year old steers and full-grown barrows and place them in fattening pens where they would be fed the corn and velvet beans John and the boys had grown that year. Soon the animals would be fat and ready to butcher. The hogs would produce many cans of lard along with the hams, shoulders and sides that they would cure and smoke. The cattle would be butchered one or two at the time and Arch would haul the meat around in the new wagon he had purchased to be sold to the people of the countryside.

Most people were anxious to purchase this meat as it was much more tender than they were accustomed to having available. The cured pork was sold mostly to the old black storekeeper who would ship the majority of it to the larger towns nearby. After several years the storekeeper began to receive requests from the city stores, asking for more of the meats from the same farm as the previous year. To keep up with the demand, Arch increased production each year by enlarging the fattening pens and fattening more animals.

They now had a very profitable operation. Before Christmas each year Arch would bring out the farm books. He, John, and the boys would sit down, and Arch would explain each entry. After they were satisfied with his explanations and had no questions, Arch would come to a settlement with them. For their work they would receive the food and other household supplies they needed during the year. After an amount for this was deducted the remaining money earned was divided. Arch took one half and the remainder was divided between John and his two boys. The money John and his sons received permitted them to steadily improve their standard of living, furnishing their home more completely each year. They now owned many things they never in their wildest imagination thought possible. Once John told Arch, "Boss, I know sometimes you might run short of money and if it ever happens you are welcome to have my savings. I know I don't have much, but you are always welcome to it anytime."

This touched Arch to know he had the trust and confidence of this black man. By treating him in the manner he himself would want to be treated had the situation been reversed, a friendship evolved between them based upon friendship and mutual trust.

No situation ever remains stable for long, however. One day as Arch rode near the field where he knew John was plowing, he heard a loud gunshot. The sound surprised him. Knowing that the boys were some distance away and had only the twenty-two rifles he had given them, he hurried to investigate. When he arrived at the field he couldn't see John, only the mule who was dragging the plow as he browsed on green briars. He discovered John lying behind some bushes, and feared that he was dead. He quickly dismounted and as he grew closer he could see John moving, attempting to stand up. His shirt was bloody and he saw that John had been shot in his right arm. He was bleeding badly and it was obvious that the shot had penetrated a blood vessel. Without hesitating Arch cut a strip from his shirt and fashioned a tourniquet, which stopped the bleeding. This was something he had done many times during the war, but did not think it would ever be necessary to repeat again. Now he knew that his knowledge of treating gunshot wounds had come in handy once again, and had probably saved John's life.

When he was sure the bleeding had stopped he helped John climb into his saddle and began leading the horse toward home. Slowly, as they traveled, John revived enough to begin telling Arch what had happened. He described the two men who assaulted him, calling them by name, and said that they were the men who ran the plantation where he had once been a slave. He said they rode up and shot him without saying a word. Arch was convinced that this was the man who had questioned him about the Negroes years before. John said they didn't say anything to him; the one who shot him just pulled his pistol and fired. Afterwards the man who shot him turned to his companion who John knew to be the plantation owner, and said, "This is one of the blacks which didn't return to the plantation. This will be a lesson he won't forget if he lives, and the others will know what they can expect if they don't do as they are told." Arch asked

John to describe the horses the men had been riding. After describing the horses, John also told Arch that both men had worn pistols that were tied down like gunfighters.

When Arch finally got John home, Sarah and John's wife treated the wound as best they knew how. Arch mounted his horse and left, riding swiftly. He went to the field where the two boys were working and told them about their father. The boys became very excited and wanted to go after the men who had shot their father. Arch ordered one of the boys to return to the house and watch for any intruders. If anyone came and attempted to bother either his sister or their mother or father he told the boy to "shoot to kill, like you have been taught to handle your rifle."

The other boy was told to unhitch Arch's mule and go to the little town and ask the doctor to come to the farm to treat John's wound. He told the boy where the doctor lived and to be on the lookout for the two men who had shot his father.

"If you see those men don't have anything to do with them," said Arch.

"I'll take care of them when we are sure your father is alright."

Neither boy questioned Arch's instructions and quickly proceeded to carry out his orders. They couldn't help but wonder what Mr. Arch intended to do. They both knew he would tell them when he wanted them to know. They had complete trust in this white man who had proven his honesty toward them many times, and who was, in reality, their mentor.

Arch returned home to make sure John was going to be all right. He then went back to the scene of the shooting, picked up the trail of the two men and began tracking them. After he had tracked them for about a mile he decided that he knew where they were heading, and he left the trail. He would attempt to intercept them at the swinging bridge that he determined was their destination.

When he arrived at the swinging bridge he found their tracks, which showed they had already crossed and were going in the direction of the little town. Knowing that they were not as familiar with the countryside as he was and would no doubt stay on the road, he decided to take a shortcut through the woods.

When he arrived in town he couldn't see their horses anywhere. He walked into the store and described the two men and their mounts to the old black storekeeper. The storekeeper said he hadn't seen them in town during the last several hours, but they had been in town earlier that morning drinking at the saloon before they left. One of them had difficulty mounting his horse and both men had been loud and vulgar in their conversation. The storekeeper had heard one tell the other, "We'll kill that black bastard and if that white son of a bitch don't like it we'll kill him, too." He said they had been talking mighty big as they rode out of his hearing. He was quite concerned but since he didn't know of whom they were speaking, he couldn't warn anyone.

Arch told the storekeeper that he intended to sit down on his porch for a little rest, and asked if it would be all right for him to move his horse around back of the store. The old man said, "Certainly. You can tie him to the rack out back. Won't anyone see him there."

When he returned, Arch sat down on the mourner's bench, laying his Sharps rifle across his lap and placing his pistol in his belt where it was readily accessible. He waited patiently. The old storekeeper knew trouble was about to occur, so he quietly closed the front door and took up watch from a window that fronted the porch.

Time passed slowly as Arch waited for the men to return. Arch knew that this could result in him being seriously hurt or perhaps killed, but this didn't weaken his resolve to settle the matter this afternoon. No longer could these two back shooters be permitted to roam about the countryside threatening anyone that didn't agree with them. He would have to prevail in the coming confrontation with these two if they were to be stopped. His mind wandered back to the war. That period in history had been different, and most men on both sides were men of principle. While they fought for different reasons in most instances and in spite of their different ideologies, they had respect for their adversaries. Of course, there had been exceptions to this rule, such as the old black sergeant at the prison camp where he and his men had been imprisoned, but men of this character were few, and seldom would troops from either side deliberately injure or kill an individual unless it was necessary to survive.

He saw the two men as they returned. When they turned down the street, riding toward him, he knew the bright sun would prevent them from seeing him sitting in the shade of the porch. When they turned their horses toward the hitching rail they would realize he was there in front of them. He had planned the confrontation this way, hoping to gain the advantage.

He was ready, and before either could dismount he said, "Well, if it isn't the two big men who go around shooting poor, unarmed Negroes who are trying to make a living." The two men showed their surprise and before either could answer Arch spoke again.

"Frankly, I don't think any man can stoop any lower, even though he is a carpetbagging son of a bitch who was sired by a low-life bastard for a father and a common whore for a mother. Don't you both agree?"

Neither of the men had seen him sitting on the porch until they reined up to the hitching post. With the sun in their eyes and facing a man with a brazen resolve, they quickly realized they were at a distinct disadvantage and in serious trouble. The man who had previously asked Arch about the Negroes stammered and stuttered, finally asking, "Are you talking to us?"

For a few moments Arch didn't respond. When he finally spoke he said, "I don't see any more shit on the street, so it should be obvious that my comments are directed to you two sorry bastards." They could now see him sitting there in the shadows, his grey eyes staring intently at them with hatred and anger. They realized they needed to defend themselves, this time from the actions of a man who had a gun and who would use it at the least provocation. They became nervous, and shifting in their saddles, they realized that dealing with this man wouldn't be as easy as the old Negro had been.

The plantation owner said, "You talk mighty big to be just one man against two. Why, we could shoot you like we did that old Negro who works for you."

This statement only further ignited Arch's temper. The higher it was he only wished he could disarm them and then beat them to death with his hands, but he knew they would never give up their guns without a fight. He said, "I am going to give you both three options and about one minute to decide which one you want to go with."

The arrogant plantation owner asked, "What options do you offer?"

Arch replied, "You can drop your guns and I'll tie you up and wait for the Sheriff to arrive, or you can ride across the street, dismount and we'll meet in the middle of the street and shoot it out. Now if neither of these options are acceptable you can pull leather where you sit and enjoy your next meal as a guest of the devil in hell. Time is up. Make your move."

At that moment, they both reached for their pistols. When the plantation owner's pistol cleared his holster he instantly met Satan as a .50 caliber rifle ball passed through and removed most of his head. The other man tried to draw his pistol, and turn his horse at the same time. As his pistol cleared the holster he tried to point his gun at Arch, but felt a .41 caliber pistol ball pass through his brain instead. Both men were dead. They fell from their horses and landed in the dirt. The storekeeper had been the only witness. It was obvious to him that Arch didn't intended to allow either of these men to leave their saddles alive, but they both drew their weapons first.

The old storekeeper peered out the door when he was certain the shooting was over. He opened the store door wide and watched as Arch walked over to the bodies and observed the damage he had done to the two men laying on the ground. After looking over the situation, the storekeeper remarked, "Well, it looks like someone should go to the depot and send a telegram to the county seat asking for the Sheriff to send a deputy to investigate a shooting."

Arch turned, looked at the old man, and said, "That might be a good job for you since you saw everything that happened." The people from the saloon came to the door and looked out. After looking over the scene they turned and went back inside, making no comment.

The storekeeper said, "I don't suppose they have any use for these two anymore since they cain't drink now."

Turning away from the bodies, Arch reached into his pocket and said, "If you cain't find someone to bury these two, take this fifty-cent piece and see if you can find someone who will drag them out in the woods where the buzzards can get to them."

He flipped the fifty-cent piece to the storekeeper as he retrieved his horse and prepared to mount. As he started to ride away he stopped and turned again to the storekeeper.

"Looks like you will have two guns and horses to sell, doesn't it? said Arch. You can tell the Sheriff what happened and if he wants to talk to me tell him where I live." With this he turned his horse and rode away.

Arriving home he found the doctor preparing to leave. He had taken care of John's wound and he told Arch, "I believe his arm be a little stiff for a few days, but in time it will straighten out. He had better take it easy for a few days, though, because he lost a lot of blood."

Arch answered, "I want to thank you for coming so promptly. Now what do we owe for your services?"

"I get two dollars for an office visit and three dollars for a house call," said the doctor, "but since this was so far from town I think you should pay me at least four dollars."

Looking at Sarah, who stood nearby, Arch said, "Sister, go to the house and get some money so I can settle up with the doctor. I spent all I had in town today.

The doctor left after he had been paid, and Arch turned to the two boys who were standing near their father. When he spoke he said, "For the next few days while your daddy is laid up you two will have to take care of all the chores. Now you boys know what has to be done. It is getting late so you might better get started. No one else will bother you."

He made no mention of the events that had occurred in town that day and no one asked any questions. They knew that when he wanted them to know he would tell them.

Several days passed and one morning just before noon a young deputy sheriff rode into the yard. Arch went outside and greeted him amicably, then invited him to come in and sit on the porch in the shade where they could talk. The young man, who looked to be about 15 years old, was a handsome fellow, about six feet tall with coal black hair and piercing black eyes, clean cut and dressed in tan pants and a light brown shirt. On his left breast was a star that indicated his position as a law enforcement officer.

After they sat down he looked at Arch and said, "You know why I've been sent here, don't you?"

Arch nodded that he did and the young man continued, "I am to make an investigation into the shooting that occurred in town in which two men were killed. I talked with the only eyewitness to the shooting, old Ike, the storekeeper, who told me you were the man who killed those two. He also said it was a clear case of self-defense. Now I also have been told that these men shot a black man that works on your farm earlier that same day and when you confronted them in town they both tried to shoot you. Is this correct?"

Arch waited for a few moments before he responded and then said, "I suppose the story you have been told is about right, but I want you to know I went to town to kill them after I found John shot in the field. They didn't say a word to him, just pulled a pistol and shot him down as he was plowing. I hope this will justify my actions."

Although he was young, the deputy was very business-like. He asked Arch several more questions seeking to understand the incident and then commented, "From what I have learned and the conversation with both you and Ike, I don't think there will be any charges made. Of course, you realize I will have to take this matter to the grand jury and their decision will determine the final outcome of the case."

"If I may I would like to ask one more question," continued the deputy. "Weren't you afraid to tackle two gunmen who had already shot one man and had bragged that if you didn't like it they would kill you also? They obviously didn't mind killing people and you were the one who stood up to them previously, isn't that right?"

Arch smiled and said, "Well Sheriff, if you had been there I would have let you handle the matter, but you weren't and someone had to stop them so I took the matter in my own hands. I am sorry it occurred, but some people think that because we are poor people they can come down here and treat us anyway they choose."

"Now, I'd like to invite you to join my sister and myself for our noon meal," continued Arch.

"I know it isn't much, but maybe it will hold you over until you ride back to the county seat."

After the young deputy had enjoyed a good country meal, he thanked them and rode away, returning to the county seat to make his report to the County Sheriff.

Later that day Arch asked Sarah to come and sit on the porch with him. As they sat he explained what happened in town that day and then said, "I hoped that I would never be called upon to kill anyone again, but those two just got me riled up. I realized they were bullies who thought they could treat people like dirt and that no one would stand up to them. When they shot John just because he wouldn't return to that plantation as their slave I intended to put a stop to their offensive ways. Just because they had a big plantation and he was a Negro didn't give them the right to try to kill him. I hope God Almighty will forgive me for what I did, but I know it was necessary. Now I hope the deputy's report will be the end of it."

With these words the matter was closed and no mention was ever made between them of this occurrence again.

16

Peace At Last?

During the next several years, calm reigned in their lives with no real problems, just the tasks of planting, cultivating, harvesting and selling the surplus crops they produced. Time soon allowed Arch and Sarah to meet their neighbors, and they enjoyed the socializing and camaraderie that evolved from the relationships that developed.

John and his family continued to live in the house Arch had built for them and grew the crops that Arch advised them to plant. While Arch chose what they would grow he left the planting, cultivating and harvesting to them. Both of John's sons were young men and they always assisted Arch in feeding the mature crops to the hogs and cattle. They would fatten them for sale each year. All surplus above what Arch and John's families needed to live was sold, and the year end distributions continued to grow. The bountiful crops and the ever-growing herds of hogs and cattle provided them with everything required for a full, rich life. Both Arch and John saved their surplus monies for that time when they might not be so lucky and funds would not be so plentiful.

Arch improved their houses by installing more glass windows, replacing the old shutters that had been used previously. One day while he was in town, Ike the storekeeper showed Arch a finely woven wire called "screen." Realizing this was a great innovation to cover their opened windows, he bought a roll and carried it home. He showed John and the boys how to make frames over which they could stretch this screen wire and place it in the windows of each house. They would no longer be bothered by the pesky mosquitoes and other insects that were so abundant in the swamp. No longer would they need to build smokes using dried cow manure to repel these insects.

Arch's life was now a very good one. As he traveled about an ever-increasing portion of the county, watching his growing herds of cattle, he would stop at each farm and discuss the weather and any problems they might be encountering. He became disturbed during some of these discussions when he learned many of the original settlers were having problems with the county government. They complained about the ever-increasing taxes, and Arch soon learned that when people were unable to pay the higher taxes, their livestock and land was being confiscated and sold to members of the county government.

He also heard rumors that his same group of county officials was issuing scrip pledging the county's credit. This was being done behind closed doors, and the same unscrupulous individuals were using this scrip to purchase many things for their personal use. As he moved about the county he heard of more and more of these acts of corruption. Many of the citizens were disturbed, and it became obvious that the seeds of rebellion had been planted. If something wasn't done to curb these practices, anarchy would ensue.

The more people he talked to the more he could see a consistent pattern emerging which indicated the members of the county government were abusing the authority granted to them by imposing on the citizen's rights. Each time an election was held the same individuals would be announced the winners. It was quite clear to many of the locals that elections were being rigged, so steps had to be taken to end this corruption.

Several of the more prominent citizens from the different sections of the county held a meeting where they discussed the problems that were facing the people of the county. They decided hold a mass protest at the courthouse so members of the county government would know of their discontent and the effect their policies were having on the people. Their hope was by working with these officials, the problems could be addressed and remedies proposed to provide relief.

The scheduled meeting was announced and all the county officials were notified of the time and place. Much to the disappointment of the large group of residents who attended this meeting, the county officials dominated the meeting and denied the local citizens the privilege of presenting their grievances. During a fiery speech by one of the officials, he refused to admit that any improper acts had been committed. He denied that scrip was being issued behind closed doors and used by officials to purchase personal items, including whiskey. He also denied that the taxes being collected were remitted to the state in amounts differing from the amounts collected. Many in attendance were aware that two sets of books were being kept, and the books that were sent to the state government differed significantly from the amounts actually being collected and remitted.

They also vehemently denied the charges including the voting irregularities and rigged elections. When an older distinguished gentleman who had been designated to respond on behalf of the citizens rose to speak, he was informed that he could not present the people's side of the issues. This action became the straw that broke the camel's back, so to speak.

Chaos broke out, and as everyone crowded down the stairs, umbrellas, walking sticks, pocket knives, and several other implements were utilized against some of the officials and their cohorts. Those people who the crowd could get to were beaten unmercifully. The doctor, who happened to be in attendance, spent the remainder of the night tending to the wounded.

Several of the more influential members of the county government barricaded themselves in a room and remained there until things calmed down. Then they slipped out of the building and left. They were unaware that all exits were being watched and each were followed to one official's home. Here they congregated to discuss their problems they now realized were quite serious. While this discussion was being held, their location was being relayed to a group of five men who had decided that this night the carpetbaggers and their cohorts would be removed from office, one way or another.

The most boastful member of the county government was a handsome man, tall, broad shouldered and well groomed. He had made the most vehement denunciation of the charges the citizens had brought against them, and was well aware he was in danger if apprehended. The people he aroused with his irritating speech would certainly be after him and no doubt would do him bodily harm if he were to be caught. So, he decided to spend the night with one of his companions and promptly sent someone to his home to bring his wife and child.

He was unaware of the meeting being held at that very moment not too far away by the five angry men. They had reached the decision that his time on this earth had expired and he was to meet his master that night, if they could get to him.

The five men who were attending this meeting were drawing straws to determine who would be delegated the privilege of assassinating him during the first opportunity that presented itself. For many years this event would be referred to as the "five man assassination." It was said that one man furnished the gun, another furnished the powder, another provided the shot, another supplied the wadding and the fifth man actually pulled the trigger and committed the murder. No one ever knew who fired the shot. The man who pulled the short straw left with the group and later returned alone to retrieve the gun and carry out the deed.

The targeted man relaxed after his wife came to the home of his friend. When he opened a shuttered window for some fresh air, he was shot dead. He was heard to say, "I have long expected this."

By morning the news of the assassination had been relayed throughout the entire county and later that morning someone heard Arch say, "There will be many dry eyes in the county this morning."

Some who heard this statement couldn't help but wonder if Arch was the assassin, but those who knew him well had never seen him with any gun except a pistol and that ever-present Sharp rifle in his saddle boot. The victim had been shot with a shotgun loaded with buckshot. Did this eliminate Arch?

No one ever knew who the assassin was except the man who pulled the trigger and his fellow conspirators.

Following this minor rebellion the remaining county officials became difficult to locate. Several left the county never to return. One was indicted on charges of robbing the U.S. Mail and was later convicted and sentenced to a term in prison. Another was the old black Sheriff, who decided to resign for health reasons and never came to the county seat again. When the turnover of the county officials had been completed, the Governor appointed a new group and the government began to run smoothly. The people who initiated the movement returned to their homes and farms, hoping to see the government operate as it should.

17

Tragedy

One day during the early spring Arch returned home after a long ride to find Sarah sitting on the porch, holding a letter and crying. This was so unusual that he immediately went to her seeking to find out the cause of the trouble. When she told him that the letter she had received was from the Preacher, their brother-in-law. His letter told of the sudden death of their sister, Mary. This sad news left both of them in shock and was very hard to accept. It caused them great sorrow and left them emotionally devastated. They just couldn't believe that such a thing could happen to their sister. They both needed solace and understanding, but knew they would have to accept it as nothing could be done to change things. They were deeply grieved and this would only to be relieved through the passage of time.

In the Preacher's letter, he asked if Sarah would come and live in his house and care for his now motherless children. To fulfill his obligations to his church he was required to travel widely in the region, serving the different churches on his circuit. Most of his time was spent away from home and he desperately needed someone he could depend on to care for his little children. If she would come and stay temporarily he would make every effort to locate someone else so she could return home.

After reading and rereading the letter several times, they mulled over the matter and finally Sarah looked at Arch and said, "Brother, it seems like every time our lives begin to look stable something unfortunate happens. I suppose I'll have to go and take care of those children until the Preacher can make other arrangements. Certainly you wouldn't want just anyone to care for them now that their mother is dead? Just as soon as firm arrangements can be made, I'll return home. In the meantime, I'm sure you can make out without me. John's wife will cook for you and take care of the house."

Arch agreed and they began discussing what would need to be done before she left. During their discussion the subject of money came up. When it was mentioned, Sarah asked Arch, "You remember the money you dug up when you returned home?"

"Yes, I gave most of it to you to keep," replied Arch.

"Do you still have it?"

"Yes," Sarah answered. "I never spent any of it except the money we gave our stepmother when she left. The balance is still hidden away safe."

Since they now had money from the operation of the farm, there was no reason to spend any of the gold money their father had hidden. Because Sarah was going away she thought that she should now divulge the hiding place of this cache. She would take enough of the farm money to make the trip and a sufficient amount to return when she felt things at the Preacher's home were stable enough.

After Sarah packed her clothes, Arch carried her to the depot that afternoon to catch the southbound train. She would have to transfer to a boat at the end of the train line that would carry her without further transfers to the Preacher's house. The trip would take about two days. The accommodations on the boat would be comfortable and afford her an opportunity to see the coastline and many other things that she had never seen. Perhaps she could sketch some of the sights and paint them later.

Following Sarah's departure, Arch realized he was destined to live alone and he became very depressed. He could depend on John's wife to cook for him and keep his house clean, taking care of his laundry and other things around the house that needed attention. But the lack of someone to keep him company when he was home left him sad. He resolved to use his spare time to move about the county more frequently, visiting people he had become acquainted with, and spend more time in the little town and the county seat.

It was during one of these excursions that something happened which would have a dramatic and lasting effect on Arch's life. In route to the county seat one extremely hot day, he became thirsty. When he came to a house he passed many times before, he wondered if the occupants would permit him to get a drink of cool water from their well which stood near the road. When he stopped, a very beautiful girl about sixteen years old came out to meet him. She was a tall girl with black hair, grey eyes, well-proportioned features, a smooth, rosy complexion, and a very pleasant smile. Dimples adorned her cheeks. When she spoke, her voice was very pleasant and she naturally showed her pearly white teeth. Her admirable beauty immediately caught his attention and after she graciously offered him the water, he attempted to prolong the conversation as long as possible to assure that she wouldn't go back into the house. During their conversation he learned that her name was Luduski. She lived with her mother and two sisters while her father spent most of his time on the coast fishing. For fear of appearing too forward, he thanked her for the water and left, but he had already made up his mind that he would see more of this young beauty in the future. Riding on to the county seat he couldn't get her off his mind. Luduski captured his thoughts and he decided that he would find a pretty gift for her in town and present it to her on his return trip. It would have to be something that she didn't already have, but since he knew so little about her, he was at a loss to decide what it should be. She was so pretty. He had to find something to impress her, but what?

When he arrived in the little town he still didn't know what he would buy for this newfound beauty, so he wandered about, looking over everything that was available in the town's two stores. Maybe he would come across something she would like. After a considerable amount of time looking over the limited merchandise in both stores, he decided that some pretty cloth with ribbon to match would make an appropriate gift. He found a bolt of cloth with a flowery pattern that he really liked and decided this was the gift he would buy for Luduski.

He asked the storekeeper, an elderly white man, "How many yards of cloth would it take to make a dress?" The merchant, visibly amused, replied, "Well, I sold a lady five yards yesterday as best I remember."

Arch thought a few moments and then asked, "How many yards are left on this bolt of material?" Before the storekeeper could reply, Arch said, "Oh, hell! Just give me all that's left and five yards of this ribbon." He chose a color that he thought would match the material.

As he returned home later that afternoon he deliberately chose the route he had traveled earlier that morning so that he would pass by Luduski's house again. As he approached, he saw her out in the yard. When he reached the gate she saw him and came to meet him.

Arch stammered and said, "I don't want any water this time, but while I was in town I saw some cloth that was so pretty I thought of you, so I bought enough for you to make a dress. There's also some ribbon to decorate it. Do you think you can have the dress made by the next time I pass? I would love to see it."

Luduski took the bundle of material from Arch and eyed it closely. Smiling, she said, "From the looks of this package you had better plan your next trip for some time in the future. If I'm not mistaken there is enough material and ribbon to make several dresses. I'll start on them in the morning."

Visably embarrassed, Arch was at a loss for words. When she saw his discomfort, she asked, "Would you like to take supper with us tonight?"

Arch stammered and finally said, "I sure would like that, if I'm not imposing on you and your family."

Luduski answered, "Well, my daddy just came in from the bay and he brought a sack of mullet and some oysters. If you like fish and oysters, you are welcome to stay and eat with us. We'll start cooking as soon as he has finished cleaning the fish."

"Where is your daddy?" Arch asked.

"Oh, he's out back," she said.

When they turned the corner Arch saw a big man standing at a high bench cleaning fish. He was a rough looking character with a heavy beard which hadn't been touched by a razor for quite a spell, long hair, dirty fingernails and barefooted. This man had the largest feet Arch could ever remember seeing attached to a human body. It looked like they had never been washed. He stood over six feet tall and when Arch introduced himself he was surprised when the man said, "Yeah, I know who you is, you is dat cow man from over the Sopchoppy River, ain't you?"

"Yes sir, I am," answered Arch.

"Your daughter has invited me to eat supper with you people tonight if it meets with your approval."

The man, who Arch later learned was named Jack, took a long look at him and finally said, "If you is gonna eat here tonight you better git yore knife and start cleaning fish. I ain't a gonna clean fish for you to eat."

As they stood at the bench cleaning fish they began to talk. Arch soon learned that Jack had been in the war also, although his services had been in the Florida Guard and hadn't been too dangerous. He had stayed out of the Federal raiders way when they made their excursions ashore to destroy the salt kettles scattered along the coast. The older man told Arch he could run across the marsh faster than any Yankee and never did they stand a chance of catching him. Arch, looking at those dirty big feet, thought "I know why they couldn't catch you." With those feet that man could almost walk on water while the raiders would bog down to their knees trying to follow him.

Soon after the fish were cleaned and washed, the aroma of frying fish permeated the area around the house. They sat around talking until they were called inside to eat. It was a very tasty meal, the delicious fish and fried oysters were served along with corn dodgers and grits. With the beautiful Luduski as a companion, what more could any man want? Perhaps the company of this girl was what Arch enjoyed most about the evening, although he had certainly enjoyed the food as well.

Later that night, as he rode along home, Arch decided to return before many days passed.

18

Courtship and Marriage

During the following few weeks Arch couldn't get Luduski off of his mind. She was constantly at the center of his thoughts and he couldn't think of anything else. His every waking moment was dominated by his thoughts of her and he would deliberately go out of his way to pass by her house. If she happened to be outside where he could see her, he would stop on the pretext of wanting a drink of water. He later confessed to her that he had never drunk as much water in his life as during this time.

When he would see her and stop, they would have long conversations. When she was not in sight, he would linger around the well hoping that she would appear. To be able to talk to her only intensified his desires, and her beauty affected him in ways nothing had ever moved him before. She was so lovely, such a beautiful girl, but there always remained his doubts that she felt anything toward him except that of being a friend. He realized the significant difference in their ages might be a stumbling block. He had great expectations that their relationship might develop into something far greater than just friendship. He realized that he was in love with her and wanted to marry her, but he didn't want to ruin things by moving too quickly and perhaps lose her if she didn't share the same feelings for him. As he rode the countryside tending to his cattle, his constant thoughts of her lead him to plan how he would approach her and reveal his love. He would ponder on it and express his feelings for her when the opportunity presented itself.

Several times when they were out walking, he attempted to tell Luduski how he felt about her, but each time he just couldn't get up the nerve and he would hesitate until the opportunity had passed. He wanted this girl in a way he had never wanted a girl before and as his desires grew stronger he decided the time must soon present itself, but when?

True, he had courted many women while in the army and following his return home. But these relationships had never brought out the intense feelings he now harbored for Luduski. It was something that had dwelled in his body for many years and now it demanded to be released.

One afternoon as they sat in the swing on the porch of her parents' home, he decided this was the time. He looked into her lovely face and asked, "Do you think the difference in our ages would prevent us from becoming more than just friends?"

Luduski smiled and said, "I don't think you are an old man,

although there is a considerable difference in our ages. Why are you asking such a question?"

He hesitated and after a few moments he said, "Well, I have grown quite fond of you over the past months. In fact, I am in love with you, and hope that you will agree to be my wife."

"Are you proposing to me?" asked Luduski.

"Yes, I am," answered Arch, "but you don't have to give me an answer right away."

"I have suspected you felt this way for some time, especially since you brought me all that cloth," she said.

"I decided a long time ago that if you were to ask me to become your wife, I would accept. You know I have strong feelings for you. I suspect we had better start making wedding plans."

After they had revealed their intentions to marry to her mother, Arch went to the bay where Luduski's father was fishing and asked for his permission to marry his daughter. The old man responded in his usual gruff manner, saying, "If you is fool enough to hook up with my girl, I can only hope and pray you both ain't making a mistake. Once you is married, there ain't no turning back. Does you understand that, cow man?"

Arch assured him that they were not making a mistake and that he was capable of providing for Luduski and the children they both hoped they would be blessed with in the years to come.

Later, when he had returned home, he sat down and wrote his sister Sarah who was still living at the Preacher's home taking care of his children. He told her of his plans to be married in the little Methodist church near the farm when the Preacher made his next trip to the church. He asked if she and the children would accompany him on this momentous occasion.

She responded with a letter expressing her happiness for him and his intended bride, wishing him a long and happy marriage. She wrote that she planned to accompany the Preacher on his next trip to the church and would bring Mary's two children who Arch had never seen. Then they would all be present at his wedding that she anticipated would be a most joyous occasion.

As the weeks passed and the time for the wedding grew nearer, there were many decisions to be made. Clothes to be made, the menu for the wedding dinner to be planned, and a host of other things that Arch never dreamed would be necessary just to get married. He realized that much food would be needed since they planned to invite the members of both families along with their children and all the neighbors and their children. They decided to have a barbecue and Arch chose a fat steer for John and his boys to butcher and cook in an open pit. John's wife would prepare different dishes several days in advance and when Sarah arrived he knew she would also get busy preparing her favorite dishes. Everyone anticipated that the wedding feast would be something to remember for many years to come.

The Preacher, his two children, and Arch's sister arrived several days before the wedding. This allowed Sarah the opportunity to get to know Luduski and also allow her sufficient time to assist John's wife in preparing the food that everyone would enjoy following the wedding ceremony.

Sarah was pleasantly surprised that such a lovely young girl had agreed to marry her brother, a man who was really old enough to be her father. She realized Luduski was settled and would make her brother a good wife. It was obvious to Sarah that the two were in love and she welcomed Luduski into the family with no reservations.

On the day of the wedding, everyone assembled at the little church for the special occasion. The church filled to capacity, and following the regular service the wedding ceremony took place. It was a simple affair that took only a few minutes and when it was over Arch invited everyone to come to the farm and help them celebrate. Tables had been placed under the large live oaks to accommodate the crowd and the bountiful food that had been prepared left little space for anything else to be placed on the tables. The barbecued beef was delicious and the other dishes, including the many pies and cakes that Sarah and John's wife had prepared, were enjoyed by all. Sarah baked a large and beautifully decorated wedding cake that now was the centerpiece of the table. Following the dinner, Arch and Luduski cut the cake and everyone enjoyed their portion.

Later, after everyone had finished eating, a group of musicians played many of the old tunes that everyone loved. Following the first dance by the bride and groom everyone joined in. Many old memories were rekindled in the older guests as some of these tunes had not been heard since they had first come to America. As the day passed, the different families socialized and mingled with their neighbors.

Soon it became time for all to return home to perform their chores before dark. The Preacher and Sarah, along with his two children, started on their journey back home and soon the married couple was left alone to begin their new life together.

19

The Good Life

In the weeks following the wedding, Arch and Luduski, who he now affectionately nicknamed "Duck," were together constantly. When it was necessary for him to ride the woods to watch over his cattle and hogs, she would accompany him, riding the old army mule he had stolen many years before. When they traveled in the direction of her parents home, they would always stop to visit and many times would enjoy a dinner with Luduski's mother and sisters. Seldom was her father home as he stayed on the coast fishing. Her mother enjoyed their visits and encouraged them to come frequently. This soon created a closely-knit family, and on those occasions when her father would return home he always brought bags of fresh mullet and oysters. For several days the entire family would enjoy feasting on these delicious foods. During the fall of the year, the mullet would be fat and filled with roe they all enjoyed. The oysters were also fat in the fall and were a scrumptious delight to eat, both fried and raw. These delicacies could also be stewed and when the stew was filled with cornbread, it made a meal they all looked forward to. Most times everyone would over eat so much they would be uncomfortable for quite some time afterward.

Following these wonderful meals at her parents' home, Arch and Luduski rode home through the woods singing and entertaining themselves with conversations about their promising future.

When the inevitable occurred and Luduski became pregnant, these excursions soon ended as she could no longer continue following him on his daily trips through the woods to tend to his stock. She remained home sewing clothes and preparing for the child they both looked forward to having.

When the time for the birth arrived, Arch sent one of John's boys for the doctor and John's wife tended to Luduski until the doctor arrived. Luduski's labor lasted for many hours with Arch nervously pacing back and forth, unable to remain still. Finally, after instructing John to send one of the boys for him if anything happened before he returned, Arch walked down to the little church.

As he entered the church, he removed his old battered hat and knelt before the altar. He offered a humble prayer to almighty God, acknowledging that he had been a sinful man during the war. He asked God to forgive him for his many sins and to permit his wife to bring their child into the world free from any impairment. He begged God to let his child be normal and promised that during the remainder of his life he would try to be a more obedient man. He also thanked God for the many blessings that he had bestowed on him and acknowledged that only through His grace had he been spared from the terrible fate that so many of his companions met during the war.

As he was preparing to leave, John burst through the church door.

"Boss!" he cried. "The missus is calling for you and wants you to come see your pretty little daughter."

Arch hurriedly left the church. He was so elated he couldn't walk fast enough and before he arrived home, he was running so fast that John said later, "I shore didn't know anything could excite that man, but when I told him he had a little girl, why he outrun me all the way home."

The child was truly a blessing to both Duck and Arch. As she grew they would sit and watch her sleeping in her cradle. Timed passed, and as she grew, so their love for her grew in proportion. Soon she began to crawl. They admired the progress she was making, and anticipated the time when she would begin to walk.

Soon Duck was pregnant again and another little girl made her appearance. Now the two proud parents had two little girls to love and enjoy. Sadly, this soon came to an end. The two daughters became critically ill with Yellow Fever. The devastated parents and concerned neighbors nursed them constantly to no avail. The condition of both girls worsened seemingly overnight; Pneumonia set in and both children died.

The parents were both devastated as they worked tirelessly to fight the fever, but to no avail. Who would have suspected that two healthy young girls could grow deathly sick and die so quickly? The parents first blamed themselves and later questioned their faith over such a tragedy. In their grief, it was their faith in almighty God and their love for each other that sustained them.

Fortunately, when this sad event occurred both the Preacher

and his sister Sarah were visiting. It was only through their support and love that Arch and Duck could sustain their sanity and continue their lives.

It was following this tragic event that Sarah told the Preacher he would have to make other arrangements for his children's care. She felt her presence was needed here to support Arch and Duck. She decided to remain and assist them during this desperate period of extreme misfortune they were experiencing. The loss of these two children was the most tragic event either had ever experienced. It would be a very long time before either of them recovered.

No longer were they the happy family that had so loved and enjoyed the two little girls as they played about the house. Although they had to go on, it was with reluctance as both were grief stricken, but resolute in their faith in almighty God.

Later, when Duck again became pregnant, they were filled with a fear that the coming child might also be taken from them. After the birth of another healthy and robust little girl, they still continued to be anxious and fearful that she too might succumb to the ailment that took the lives of their other little girls. They did not let her out of their sight until it became obvious that this healthy child would not die as her two sisters had.

In time, there were more children born to Arch and Duck. Soon the family consisted of one girl and five boys. Arch remarked on the day his fifth son was born, "It is odd that today my fifth son is born and I am fifty-seven years old. My father was fifty-seven when I was born. I think of him many times and only wish that he could see the many blessings that have been bestowed upon his own son."

Through the years Arch's children grew, his crops were bountiful, his stock continued to multiply, and life was good. The cattle ranged further from home as the herds grew and soon it was necessary for him to devote more and more of his time to riding the woods, caring for and protecting his animals. It became a familiar sight to see Arch riding his horse through the countryside, always with his rifle across the saddle, ever watchful for anything or anyone who might be intent on bringing harm to or stealing his stock.

John and his boys now handled the crops on the farm, planting, cultivating and harvesting, always under the watchful eye of Arch. He would ride long distances in his effort to protect and care for his ever-increasing herds, and it sometimes required him to spend many nights in the woods camping. His reputation as a good and fair man became known by all he met.

Many years later, one of Arch's grandsons asked a little old lady, who was approaching her one hundredth birthday, if she had known his grandfather.

"Yes," she said, "I knew him well. He was a good man. He allowed my family to pen his cattle for the fertilizer and if any of the cows were fresh we could milk them, if we could get them in a break and separate the calf during the night. Many times he would come by our house asking about his cattle and occasionally he would spend the night in our home."

The amusing thing about this lady's comments was that she was ninety-nine years old when she said this and Arch had already been dead over ninety years. It was truly amazing that his kindness had fostered this impression on the lady who was only a mere child when she had known him.

Many changes occurred over the years. Sadly, John died, and his family said they could no longer live on the farm, as the familiar surroundings were a constant reminder of him. They soon moved away. This resulted in the crops being reduced to much less acreage and now the volume produced hardly fed Arch's family, and left no surplus to be sold. With Arch's health deteriorating, he could no longer farm the fields. His boys were too small and he could now only manage a small herd of cattle.

It was impossible for one man to maintain the operation that had been so successful and soon their livelihood became limited. When the price of cattle dropped they spent all the surplus money that had been accumulated during the good years. The expanded family required more and more to sustain a limited lifestyle. Soon, they were almost destitute. Though Arch had many acres of land and many head of cattle, neither produced much income and times for the family became very hard.

20

An Instance of Temper

It was during the summer, when the weather was very hot and extremely humid, the time when corn was in the roasting ear stage and made a very desirable food. Arch decided to send his oldest son Angus, who was named for his grandfather, to a small field he had planted for the family's use. He instructed Angus to saddle the riding mule and take a burlap bag with him to the field and break four dozen ears, cautioning him to be sure the ears he broke were not too hard. This would be a part of their noon meal that day and he looked forward to having both boiled corn on the cob and some of the corn creamed and fried.

When Angus returned with the bag of corn, he informed his

father that the neighbor's bull had torn their fence down and was out in the middle of the corn patch filling his belly on their corn. Arch hadn't been in the best of health and this corn patch had been all his health permitted him to plant and cultivate that year. To learn that Samson's old bull was eating his corn after he had asked his neighbor several times to do something about the nuisance bull made him extremely angry. After thinking about it for several minutes, Duck, who had heard the boy's report and saw the evidence of her husband's anger, she attempted to calm him down, but to no avail. Arch turned to his son and said, "Go hitch the wagon and bring it to the house." Then, turning to his second son, called "Little Arch", he said, "Go get my new rifle and be damn sure it is fully loaded."

Both boys immediately proceeded to carry out their father's wishes. Duck, knowing there was little chance of changing his mind once it had been made up, said, "Please don't do anything rash." But he knew what he planned to do, and when the wagon was ready, Little Arch stood holding the new lever action rifle his grandfather had given his father as a gift. Duck now knew there would be trouble if he encountered the bull or its owner, but there wasn't anything she could do to stop him. She could only pray that nothing bad would happen. Arch climbed into the wagon and turning to the two larger boys said, "You two older boys climb in. I may need you." With these comments, the boys climbed into the wagon and they rode away in the direction of the field.

21

The Death of a Bull

As they rode toward the field, Arch's thoughts were on the only patch of corn he had successfully been able to plant. A damn nuisance bull was destroying the crop, though Arch asked the owner on several occasions to stop him. Had it been one of his bulls in his neighbor's garden, he would have taken care of the matter even if it meant destroying the animal. He wouldn't let one of his animals bother his neighbor's property. Now he would have to kill this bull and no doubt there would be hard feelings. He hated to have contention with his neighbor, but he refused to let that damn bull tear apart his corn patch. He would have to act in his own behalf, and if that bull was in his corn patch, he was going to do what the owner should have done. He was going to kill the animal and stop him from destroying people's fences.

When he arrived at the field and saw the broken fence, his temper rose to an even higher degree. He watched the bull moving methodically about in the center of the corn patch breaking down stalks, biting into an ear of corn and slowly eating it only to go to another stalk and repeat himself. The bull appeared to be enjoying Arch's corn better than he would have had it been his owner's corn. This quickly ignited Arch's temper and when he stood up in the wagon, he calmly took careful aim and shot the bull, killing him instantly. The two boys were amazed that their father could kill the bull with one shot from that distance. Neither uttered a word as they watched their father. They realized he was angry and had no intention of redirecting his wrath toward them. As Arch sat down he turned to his youngest son and said, "Little Arch, I want you to go through the woods to Samson's house and tell him I shot his bull in my corn patch. If he wants to come and get him, tell him you boys will help him skin and load the bull. You also tell him I'll be at the house if he wants to see me."

Later, when Little Arch returned, he told his father, "That old son-of-a-bitch was mad as hell about you killing his damn bull. He said he was going to the depot and telegraph the sheriff requesting a warrant for your arrest. That was one mad old bastard."

Arch couldn't help but smile as he listened to the boy and when he had finished telling of his encounter with Samson, Arch asked, "Boy, where in the hell did you learn to swear like that?"

Realizing what he'd said, Little Arch was now visibly shocked that his father had heard him talk in such a manner. He responded, "Pa, you know you talk like that every time you get mad. Why, I have heard much worse than that when you were mad at a cow or hog."

Not to belabor the point, Arch said, "Don't let me hear you talk like that in front of your mother again. That's man talk and we'll keep it away from the house, do you understand?"

"Yes sir," the boy answered, knowing full well not to ignite his father's temper again that day.

Arch sat down in his chair on the porch and thought about what Little Arch had reported. He turned to Duck, who sat at his side and said, "That old bull has tried my patience and I'm not sorry that I killed him, the damn nuisance. He has torn down more fences than he was worth and if I hadn't killed him I'm sure someone else would have done so later. Since I'm the one that killed him, then I'll have to bear the blame, but I don't intend to go to Samson and beg for forgiveness. I'll just wait and see what comes of it. If one of my cows had caused someone the trouble that old bastard has caused me, why I would have killed it years ago. I guess if they get a warrant for my arrest I'll just have to go to jail because I don't have money for a bond nor to hire a solicitor to defend me. If I should be found guilty and be fined, I'll just have to serve jail time."

His oldest son, Angus, was standing nearby. "Pa," he said, "you know you cain't go to jail. Your health ain't as good as it was when the damn Yankees put you in jail after the war. You need Ma to take care of you and if it comes to someone serving time in jail I'll say I killed the damn bull and serve the time for you."

"Well, you are right about my health," said Arch, "but they already know I killed the damn bull so we'll just have to wait and see what comes of it. I do appreciate your offer, but you know they wouldn't let you serve time for me."

Sometime later, Arch told Angus and Little Arch, "You had better go down to the field and fix the fence where the bull tore it down. If Samson is there getting his bull, offer to help, but don't say anything to rile him up. I would hate to have to kill the old son-of-a-bitch if he caused you boys any trouble. If he starts a conversation just answer his questions politely, but don't volunteer any information. Do you all understand?"

"Yes Pa," Angus answered, "we understand." He and Little Arch started toward the barn with the three younger boys following closely behind. When they returned in the wagon, Arch could see they had loaded axes, shovels, and fence stretchers along with several pieces of web wire and new lightered posts. Arch asked, "Did you remember to carry nails and staples?"

"Yes sir," Angus replied.

Arch told the three younger boys they couldn't go with their brothers, and their disappointment registered on their faces. Neither argued with their father, however, knowing that his mind would not be changed.

After the boys had left for the field, Duck, who had remained silent until the larger boys were out of earshot, turned to Arch and quietly said, "You know that temper of yours is going to get you in trouble one of these days if it hasn't already done so."

"Well, yes, I expect it will if I live long enough," said Arch, "but don't count on this being the time."

Much later that afternoon the boys returned from the field. They told Arch that while they were repairing the fence, Mr. Samson had come to get the dead bull. They said he had brought three of his sons to help him skin the bull and they had also helped load the bull after they had finished skinning him. Little Arch, who was about ten years of age, asked, "Pa, do you think they is gonna eat that dead bull?"

"No," said Arch. "I expect they will boil him in the syrup kettle and feed the meat to the dogs and hogs, but it would be perfectly alright to eat the meat if they wanted to. He probably wanted the hide to tan, and it will make some fine leather."

"Well Pa," the boy continued, "do you think he'll tan the tail, too?"

"Probably, but why are you asking such a question, boy?" asked Arch.

"Well," said Little Arch, "I was thinking that the end of that old bull's tail would make a fine cracker for my whip and I was gonna ask him the next time I see him if'n I could have it."

"Son, I don't think under the circumstances you'd better ask for any part of that damn bull," said Arch. "It's probably going to be pretty expensive for me as it is."

The next day, as the sun had about reached its zenith, Arch sat on his porch and watched as a rider came up the road leading to his house. Since visitors were very few he had a pretty good idea who this would be, and soon his speculation was confirmed. It was the handsome young deputy sheriff on his big black horse.

As he rode into the yard, the deputy turned and went to the hitching rail that stood just outside the yard fence. He dismounted and tied his horse. When he turned toward the house, Arch greeted him and he responded in a most friendly manner, smiling broadly. Arch invited him to sit on the porch where it was cool.

Before the deputy could state his business, Arch said, "I've been expecting you or your boss and I know what your business is."

The young deputy was the same one who had come to see him several years before when he had killed the two men who had shot John, his Negro farmer. Now he was a full grown man, at least six foot tall, with black hair neatly combed, black piercing eyes that fairly sparkled, and a dark complexion, tanned to indicate he spent much time out in the sun, no doubt

153

going about the county serving warrants and other legal papers for the court.

He wore a black felt hat with a wide brim, and Arch couldn't help but see the black handle of a pistol protruding from a holster on his belt. The crease in his tan trousers indicated they had been worn very little since they had left a smoothing iron. On his shirt over the left breast was a gold star that had the words, "Deputy Sheriff" clearly embossed to identify his official position.

As he turned from the hitching rail the deputy asked, "Have you been ill? I haven't seen you about the county lately."

Waiting until they were seated on the porch, Arch replied, "Well, I haven't been bed sick, but I have been poorly lately and haven't traveled much. I expect I'll have to do a little traveling now though since I know what brings you out this way."

"I do have a warrant for your arrest," said the deputy, "but since you are not feeling good I expect you and I can work something out and you won't have to go to jail." He continued, "This warrant alleges that you killed your neighbor's bull yesterday. Since I can see you are sick I'll agree to let you stay home if you will agree to be in the county seat on the first Monday of next month when the court will be in session. I'll just tell old man Bob the sheriff to expect you in court when it convenes."

"Young man," began Arch, "you are a most accommodating fellow, and if you will let me stay home and not have to go to jail, I will give you my sole promise to be in court as requested to answer these charges provided the Lord lets me live, and I am able to make the trip."

"Now with subject settled, how about you telling me what happened," said the deputy.

Swatting at a yellow fly with the palmetto fan he had in his hand, Arch looked at the deputy and said, "I've been under the weather for several days and my wife has been giving me some medicine, but it hasn't helped much. I suppose all those years of dragging around the country during the war and the hard life I have spent since, staying out in the woods about half the time, has had a bad effect on me. But getting back to what happened yesterday, I can only tell you that had I not been sick I probably wouldn't have killed Samson's old bull. He was a huge animal and on several occasions he had destroyed my fences. He just went where he wanted to regardless of how good a man's fence might be. Yesterday I sent my oldest boy to the field to get a mess of roasting ears for our dinner and when he returned with the corn he told me that damn old bull had torn down my fence and was in the middle of my little patch of corn filling his belly. I just let my temper get the best of me and I had the boys hitch my wagon and carry me to the field. When we got there I looked at the damage that old bastard had done to my fence. When I saw him standing there in the middle of my corn patch, steadily tearing down my corn, it was more than I could take and I killed him."

"I didn't want him to go to waste so I sent one of my boys over to Samson's house to tell him what I had done so he could come and get the bull,"Arch continued.

"When my son returned he told me that Samson was going to get a warrant for me for killing his bull and apparently that is what he did or you wouldn't be here. If I had known he would feel that way I would have had the boys hitch the mule to the bull and dragged him to the river and let the gators have a feast on him."

The deputy smiled and indicated by nodding his head that he agreed. He asked if one of the boys could accompany him to the field so he could see the fence the bull had torn down, and where Arch had killed the bull.

Angus volunteered to accompany the deputy, and after he had saddled the riding mule they left.

About an hour later they returned and as it was well past time for the noon meal, Duck invited the deputy to share their late dinner and he immediately accepted, remembering the last time he had eaten with them and the good food she had served. He anticipated another good meal and as usual their table was piled high with a simple fare that most country folks enjoyed. The deputy, being a country boy himself, enjoyed this meal as much as he had the previous time.

After finishing their meal, the deputy and Arch sat on the porch for a brief visit and soon the deputy, knowing he had several more stops to make, thanked them for their hospitality and announced that he would be on his way as he had papers to serve on the way home. As he mounted his horse to leave he turned to Arch and said, "I'll be seeing you in town next first Monday."

The old man replied, "I'll be there." With these parting remarks the deputy rode away.

Late that afternoon the deputy arrived back in the county seat and found the courthouse closed. Knowing that the sheriff would be at home, he rode to the sheriff's house, which was only a short distance from the courthouse. He was greeted by the sheriff who was sitting on his porch attempting to find a cool breeze that might provide relief from the terrible heat. He greeted the deputy by asking, "Well, did you get the old man?"

"Well, yes and no", the deputy replied.

"You see, I didn't have any trouble finding him, but the old man has been sick and wasn't able to travel, so I agreed to let him stay at home until the first Monday of the month when court convenes. I know this is a little unusual, but circumstances had to be considered. I hope this meets with your approval."

Smiling as he responded, the sheriff said, "Son, you know I trust your judgment and knowing the old man I think you made a wise decision. If it comes to it we can always go back and get him, but by leaving him at home, he will receive the good care necessary for him to improve. I'm sure he will be here when court convenes next month. Now you'd better go home and get your supper and some rest. I know you are tired and hungry."

Hearing this the deputy decided he wouldn't mention that he had enjoyed a very good meal at Arch's house, but he did look forward to getting home and seeing Babe and their boys.

The sheriff laughed to himself as the deputy rode away, knowing that Arch wouldn't let that boy go hungry. He decided he wouldn't mention it unless the deputy told him he had eaten with Arch and Duck.

22

The First Trial

The first Monday of the month following the killing of the bull arrived with the weather hot, sultry and humid. As the sheriff and his deputy approached the courthouse that morning, they both had some apprehension that the old man might not show up. They had discussed the matter on several occasions, and each time the deputy had assured the sheriff that Arch would be there on the first Monday. But now that the time had arrived, he really wasn't sure.

Upon their arrival at the courthouse, both men were pleasantly surprised to see Arch's wagon tied to the hitching rail and his saddle horse tied to the rear of the wagon. They greeted the old man and his wife, who had accompanied him, and invited them both to come in the sheriff's office for a cup of coffee. Nothing was said about the impending trial during their conversation.

Just before the appointed hour for court to convene, they all went into the courtroom and were seated. The Judge entered and promptly called court into session. The Judge, a short man with a white mustache and long, white, flowing hair that reached to his shoulders, was dressed in a long white coat, vest, white shirt and a black string tie. He made a most impressive figure. He had served as a colonel in the Confederate army and was known to be partial to former Confederate soldiers.

After several other cases had been settled by a variety of defendants who pleaded guilty and were sentenced, the Judge called Arch's case and asked how he wanted to plead. Arch rose humbly, holding his battered hat in his hand and answered, "Well Judge, I killed Samson's bull, but I think the circumstances warranted the action I took."

The Judge thought for a few moments before he responded, saying, "I believe if you have reservations about the action you took you should plead not guilty and let a jury decide if you are justified in your actions or if you should be penalized."

"If that is what you think I should do," said Arch, "then I will plead not guilty, but I did kill the bull."

"I appreciate your honesty, but I am of the opinion that it is best to let a jury decide the guilt or innocence of the defendant," said the Judge.

"Mr. Clerk, call a venue and let's get this trial started."

The clerk arose and after placing his glasses on his nose began to read from a list of registered voters, calling six men by name. When they were seated the Judge asked, "Do any of you men have any reason you cain't serve on this jury?"

Two men stood up, indicating they thought they had a reason not to serve. When the Judge asked what their reasons were, one responded that he hauled oysters to Georgia and his wagon was loaded and parked in the shade outside. If he had to wait until the trial was over, his ice would be melted and his oysters would spoil before he could reach his destination in Georgia. The other man said his wife was expecting and since he had been present at the laying of the keel, he thought he should be present when the boat was launched.

After the laughter had subsided, and only a few snickers remained, the Judge dismissed these two after giving them a stern lecture on their responsibility as good citizens. In the end, he warned the oyster hauler that if he wasn't careful, he was going to kill some of those dumb Georgia crackers, selling them oysters in a month that didn't have an "R" in it. The clerk called two more citizens to the jury box and after the Judge, the prosecutor, and the individual who was going to defend Arch had questioned them, the trial began. The last two jurors selected told the Judge they certainly appreciated the opportunity to serve because they could use the two-dollar fee they would receive for this service.

The trial then began with the prosecutor first calling the deputy, who testified that he had served the warrant and the defendant had been very nice to him, even feeding him a good dinner. Later he said that one of Arch's sons had accompanied him to the field to see where the bull had torn down the fence. He said the boy showed him where his father had been in the wagon when he shot the bull and it had no doubt been a most impressive shot considering the distance, which he had estimated to be approximately two hundred yards. He didn't know many men who could kill a bull cleanly at that distance. He had also observed that the bull had been removed, leaving only a considerable amount of blood and the guts in the field. Further, the boy stated that Mr. Samson came and skinned the bull and he and his brother had assisted Samson's sons in loading the skinned bull into Samson's wagon. Samson then left, going toward his home.

The deputy further testified that after he left Arch's home, he had gone to Samson's house and observed the dead bull being boiled in the syrup kettle. They had shown him the hide that was being soaked in a barrel of brine. He had the bull's owner remove the hide from the brine and upon inspection he had identified the brand to be the same brand Samson had registered at the county clerk's office. He had noted that the bull had been shot between the eyes and ears in the center of his head and it was obvious to him that the bull must have died instantly.

The prosecutor questioned his decision to allow the defendant to remain at home after he had been arrested, and the deputy responded, "When I observed the physical condition of Mr. Arch, I reached the conclusion that he needed to remain home where his wife could wait on him and provide treatment necessary for him to recover. I had no doubt that if he was physically able when the trial was held he would be present. You can see that my trust was not misplaced."

The man chosen to defend Arch, while not an attorney, had been selected by the Judge because he had served as a Judge Advocate in the Confederate army and no one else had any legal experience.

When he began to question the deputy, it quickly became apparent that the Judge didn't approve of the questions being asked. He made several attempts to divert the jury's attention from the facts being brought forth for their consideration. He didn't want the jury to realize that the bull that had been killed had been a rogue who had destroyed the property of many of the citizens of the area. It now appeared that he wanted the jury to find Arch guilty.

Arch's defender attempted to show the jury that the bull had destroyed the fence around Arch's field of corn and had entered and eaten the corn planted inside the fence. When he asked the deputy if the fence had been in good condition, the Judge refused to allow the deputy to respond to the question. After several attempts to show that Arch had been provoked by the bull destroying his crop, the defender gave up and permitted the deputy to leave the witness box.

Next, Samson was called and stated that he had been told by Arch's son that Arch had killed his bull. When he went to Arch's field, he found the dead bull exactly as the boy had described him.

Again, the defense was brief, only asking if Samson had been aware that his animal was destroying his neighbor's property. He said that yes, several had complained, but his bull was a fine animal and he hadn't wanted to get rid of him because he sired very good calves.

The prosecutor then rested his case and the defense asked if anyone could testify that they had seen Arch kill the bull.

Realizing that he had made a grave error, the prosecutor asked the Judge to allow the prosecution to reopen the case, but the Judge responded by saying that he didn't think that would be necessary since Arch had admitted that he killed the bull.

Noting that the noon hour was fast approaching, the Judge announced that court would be in recess and would resume after dinner at two o'clock. When the Judge left the courtroom, he was accompanied by Samson and they were carrying on a very serious conversation.

Much speculation was beginning to be made as to the outcome of the trial and if it would be a fair decision. Members of the jury quickly left the courthouse and several of them were observed going in the direction of the Judge's home.

Following the recess, when court was called back into session, it soon became apparent to those seated in the courtroom that this case had been decided outside the courtroom and in all probability at the Judge's house during the noon recess.

After the Judge had instructed the jury on the legal points of the law he concluded his statements by instructing them to retire and reach a decision. Instead of leaving the courtroom they quickly announced that a decision had been reached.

Those watching the expression on Samson's face could tell that the jury's verdict would be guilty. It was obvious that the Judge had given the jury orders to find Arch guilty while they were having dinner at his house. The Judge asked the jury to announce the verdict.

Rising, the foreman of the jury avoided looking toward Arch and said, "Judge, you know, and all members of the jury know, Arch killed Samson's bull, but the prosecution didn't prove it. Now we wouldn't say guilty if Arch hadn't been honest and said here in court that he killed the bull. This wouldn't have been necessary if Samson had done something with that damn bull when his neighbors complained, but he didn't take any action and Arch killed the damn bull while he was eating his corn. I guess what I'm saying is the verdict is guilty."

The Judge sat back in his chair and appeared to be pondering the verdict. After a few moments he declared that he was now ready to impose sentence on Arch. Meanwhile those in the courtroom could see the smug expression on Samson's face and they now knew their speculation on what had transpired during the noon recess was being carried out.

Arch arose when the Judge asked him to stand. The Judge, looking toward the rear of the courtroom, said, "Arch, the jury has convicted you of killing Samson's bull. Now I could sentence you to serve time in jail. However, since you are in poor health, I am going to sentence you to pay Samson ten dollars for the bull and caution you to control your temper. I am aware that you were an officer in the Confederate army, as I was, but this does not give you any latitude to fail to observe the law and the restrictions it places on the citizens of this state. Court is adjourned."

Arch stared at the Judge as he hurriedly gathered his papers and left the courtroom. It was obvious the Judge didn't want to look Arch in the face, and Arch's expression indicated his displeasure. After a few moments, he reached into his pocket and, producing a shiny ten dollar gold piece, threw it on the clerk's desk. He turned and spoke in a clear voice that could be heard throughout the courtroom by everyone present, including the Judge, who was exiting the room as hurriedly as he could.

Arch said, "I recognize the verdict was correct. However, it was not reached by the jury, but rather by a very biased Judge. I did kill the bull, but the sentence imposed was unfair. Why, everyone present in this courtroom knows a damn cow isn't worth but fifty cents and I'll have to sell twenty cows to pay this fine. I know why the Judge was so unreasonable, and it wasn't the crime. He just wanted everyone to recognize that he was a colonel in the army and he can make an example of me because I was just a little second lieutenant. But I got my bars on the field of battle and not because of my political ability at a headquarters unit. He didn't even get close enough to battle to smell the burning powder nor hear the whine of a bullet as it passed by his head. I spent six months in a Yankee prison because I don't let people force me to do anything that I don't want to. So, let this be a lesson to all you little people, don't let anyone run over you and remember you can fight back at the ballot box when the next election is held."

When he had finished his statement, everyone there realized this was a mad man. No one, including the sheriff or his deputy, wanted to cross him today for many had heard how he had killed two heavily armed men in a shootout after they shot his Negro farmer. Because of his ability with both a rifle and pistol, everyone knew he wasn't a man to be crossed when he was angry and no one could say with certainty whether or not he had that deadly pistol under his overall jumper. Everyone knew the damage he could do with that rifle if provoked, as well.

The Judge wanted everyone to think he hadn't heard Arch's remarks criticizing his decision, and Arch's denunciation of his position in the Confederate army, and how he received his commission. He quickly left the courthouse, climbed into his buggy and began to viciously apply his whip to his unfortunate animal. One of the bystanders who had witnessed everything that had been said was heard to comment, "Poor horse. He didn't put that old hypocrite in his place, but he'll have to take the whipping because I'll bet the Judge won't ever say one word to Arch and will stay as far away from him as possible."

Arch and Duck left the courthouse and slowly walked to the hitching rails. After Arch had helped her into the wagon, he untied the mule and climbed into the wagon beside her. They started in the direction of their home and those watching observed the saddled horse tied to the rear of the wagon and noted the ever-present rifle protruding from the scabbard on the saddle.

As the wagon moved slowly along the road toward their home, Arch didn't say anything. Duck knew he was angry and as they rode along he was mulling over in his mind the events of the day. She tried to talk to him, but he wouldn't respond and soon she lapsed into silence. They had traveled several miles before he finally spoke. "Duck, you know I killed that damn bull and I had every right to take that action, but that old Judge wasn't fair imposing the fine he did and he knew it. He could have fined me the true value of the bull and the cost of court. But no, instead he wanted everyone to know he was a big man in the army and still feels like he is a colonel. Why, I doubt he ever saw any action except from behind his desk. Never did he fight in a battle. He was just a politician with money who could buy a position and play the big shot."

Duck replied, "Just because you were a mere lieutenant, you think he wanted to show you he was more important than you were?"

"He thought I didn't have any money, so he would fine me real heavy and I wouldn't be able to pay, then he could put me in jail to show his importance," said Arch. "Well, I gave the clerk the last ten dollar piece my Pa left me and its going to be a long time before I forget how I was treated. You can count on me getting even if it takes the rest of my life."

Early the next morning, the telegraph operator at the depot was busy sending and receiving messages when he suddenly jumped up and ran out of the depot. He stopped across the street from the depot where a group of men were sitting on the mourner's bench in front of the local store. He excitedly asked if anyone had heard the news.

No one had any idea what he was talking about, so one of the men asked, "What in the hell are you talking about? You know you are the only one with any contact outside of town and nothing has happened here."

The excited telegrapher answered, "I just received a message from the station up the line near the county seat and I was told that the county courthouse burned down last night."

"Wonder how that happened?" one of the men asked.

"Well, you know what that means, don't you?" one of the other men replied.

"We'll have to pay more taxes to replace it."

In the county seat there was much excitement and speculation about how the fire had gotten started. Several theories were being advanced, one being that someone attending the trial the previous day had probably thrown a lighted cigarette down and it had smoldered until it set the fat lightered building on fire.

167

Others thought that the origin of the fire would never be known, but one individual, the deputy, didn't say anything. He began to look around, trying to determine what had actually started the fire. Out in a little strip of woods near the burned out building he discovered a new kerosene can bearing the logo of one of the local stores.

It didn't strike him right that someone would throw away a new kerosene can. Finding it so near the burned out building only led him to believe that he might have discovered why the courthouse had burned. Taking the can to the store whose logo had been pasted to its outside, he casually asked the storekeeper if he had sold any kerosene cans lately like this one he was displaying.

Without hesitation the storekeeper answered, "Yes, why yesterday just before dark I sold a gallon can of kerosene to Arch. He said that he had to hurry home because they were out of kerosene and his wife couldn't have a light until he got back."

Realizing that he might be onto something, the deputy cautioned the storekeeper not to mention their conversation, and he continued his investigation. After thinking about the time the kerosene had been sold and remembering that old Uncle Pat Aligood always sat on his porch facing the courthouse each afternoon after he had his supper to smoke his pipe, he decided to wander over and have a talk with the old man. Remembering that Arch and Pat were close friends who had been in the war together, he would have to be very careful not to let on that he might suspect Arch was possibly the cause of the fire.

He waited until he knew Mr. Aligood would have finished his supper and would be sitting on his porch enjoying his pipe, before he walked over. After greeting the old man and sitting down in one of the empty porch rockers, he casually mentioned the hot weather and several other insignificant items. Then he asked if Mr. Aligood had been sitting on his porch the previous afternoon.

"Why, yes," the old man answered.

"I sit on my porch every afternoon enjoying my pipe. My wife doesn't like for me to smoke in the house, so when the weather is pleasant, you can always find me here."

The deputy then asked, "Did you see anything unusual yesterday before the fire?"

"No, I cain't think of anything," said Aligood.
The deputy then asked, "Did you see anybody pass by?"

The old man thought for several minutes before he answered, then he said, "Yes, I did see Arch."

"What was he doing?" asked the deputy.

"Why, it was near dark and he was going towards the courthouse, I suspect to get his horse. It looked like he had a kerosene can in his hand and was probably going home."

After a few minutes had lapsed and their conversation wandered about the deputy told Mr. Aligood he suspected he had better be going home because Babe probably had his supper cooked and on the table. It provoked her if he wasn't there ready to eat when she got it cooked."

Leaving the old man he went directly to the sheriff's home to report what he had discovered. After he had disclosed his findings to the sheriff, they discussed the possibility, and reached the conclusion that the deputy had discovered the cause of the fire that had burned the courthouse.

The sheriff and the deputy did not disclose their findings to anyone and waited until the next session of the grand jury that occurred several weeks later. Their disclosure to the grand jury came as a complete surprise to everyone. The grand jury indicted Arch, charging him with the crime of arson, the burning of the county courthouse. A warrant was issued and the following day the sheriff and the deputy went to Arch's farm to serve the warrant and arrest him. He greeted then most cordially, inviting them in and appeared to be genuinely surprised when they disclosed their mission. Arch was permitted to change his clothes before they escorted him to the county jail.

Early the next morning, Duck, along with their oldest son Angus, appeared at the courthouse and inquired what Arch's bond had been set at. They told her that the Judge had set Arch's bond at one thousand dollars knowing this sum would be far in excess of any money Arch's family could raise. The Judge had told the sheriff that he was setting the bond high enough that Arch wouldn't be able to post it and he would keep him in jail. Much to the surprise of the sheriff and the deputy when they told her the amount necessary to get Arch released she opened her pocketbook and removed a large roll of bills. She counted out one thousand dollars and then turned to the sheriff and said, "Turn Arch out."

When Arch had been released, he appeared as surprised as the sheriff and the deputy, and after they had left the jail, he turned to Duck and asked, "Woman, where in the hell did you get all that money?"

She smiled and walked several steps toward the wagon where their son sat. She turned to Arch and said, "You didn't think for a minute that Pat Aligood would let you stay in jail if it was in his power to get you released, did you?"

"He rode to our house last night and told me he probably was the reason you were charged. During a conversation with that young deputy he revealed that he had seen you on the afternoon of the fire going toward the courthouse with a kerosene can in your hand. When he had served under you for four years and then walked from New Jersey with you after the damn Yankees had released you three from that military prison, there wasn't any way you were going to stay in jail if he could prevent it. Pat said he had plenty of money and if he couldn't use it to get you released it wouldn't be any good."

"Well, that is what you could call a true friend, isn't it?" said Arch.

"Now Arch, we have to go by Pat's house and return the rest of the money that wasn't required to get you out of jail," said Duck.

"Just how much money did Pat give you?" asked Arch.
She smiled. "Five thousand dollars," she said. "He wanted me to have enough and we thought that would be adequate."

23

The Second Trial

Circuit Court in Florida, which handles all felony cases, is held at six-month intervals in each county of the circuit. Since the recent term of Circuit Court in Wakulla County had just been terminated, it resulted in Arch's trial pending for almost six months. During this time at the insistence of Pat Aligood, Arch went to the State Capitol in Tallahassee. After discussing his case with several of his friends from his Civil War days, he hired a distinguished lawyer named Long to defend him in the forthcoming trial. Pat Aligood had accompanied him and assured Arch that whatever the cost, he would loan him the necessary money. The county was confronted with a problem since there was no courthouse in which a trial could he held and the weather would be severely cold at the time of the next session of Circuit Court in Wakulla County.

Following negotiations with the adjacent county, it was decided that the trial would be held in the county seat of the State Capitol in Tallahassee. There were many veterans of the Civil War residing in the area and there was much discussion between them about whether or not Arch would receive a fair trial or be sent to prison. Many of the veterans made no bones about their opposition to this outcome. This was one of their comrades who had been an outstanding individual, and rose from the rank of private to become an officer in the Confederate army. Those who had served under him during the war were determined that he would receive a fair trial; otherwise there could be a minor rebellion. Several who planned to attend the trial intended to be armed, and expressed their intent to assure a fair trial, even if it required them to take severe action.

It soon became apparent to the Court that there would be a large crowd of Civil War veterans present and every effort must be taken to assure a fair trial that would prevent these men from rebelling.

After learning of the opposition to him conducting the trial, the local judge from Wakulla County decided it would be too dangerous for him to preside over this case. Most everyone felt that his action in the prior trial had contributed to the burning of the courthouse. He requested the Chief Judge of the Circuit to permit him to step down and allow another to be appointed to handle the case. It was decided that the Circuit Judge assigned to Leon County would conduct the trial. His reputation for being a fair and unbiased judge who would not tolerate disruption and would maintain his court in an orderly manner was perhaps the reason he was chosen.

The morning of the trial the courtroom was filled to capacity and many of those who couldn't find a seat stood around the walls of the courtroom. Most of those attending were former members of the Confederate army, as one of their comrades was on trial. One of the most vocal individuals was a man named Amos, who lived a considerable distance from the site of the trial. Lacking a horse, he had walked several miles that morning in the dark to assure that he had a seat in the courtroom. He was an extremely large man, almost seven feet tall, and weighing around three hundred pounds. When he spoke, his voice was a deep bass that could be heard throughout the courtroom. His seat was on the front row near the outside wall of the building. On the opposite side of the courtroom sat another former veteran of the Confederate army named Zeke, a small man barely five feet tall and weighing about one hundred pounds. He was an acquaintance of Amos, and before the trial began they called across the courtroom to each other several times discussing different things.

When the judge entered the room and called court into session the room became very quiet. Perhaps this resulted from the Judge's reputation for being strict. Everyone knew that on several occasions he had jailed individuals who disrupted his court.

The trial began with an admonishment from the Judge notifying everyone present that he would not tolerate any disruptive behavior or any comments from anyone except the prosecutor, the defense attorney, and the witnesses. He then asked the clerk to read the charges after asking Arch to stand. When the clerk finished reading the indictment, the Judge looked at Arch and his attorney who stood beside him and asked, "How do you plead?"

In a loud clear voice that could be heard throughout the courtroom Arch answered, "I plead not guilty."

Turning to the clerk the Judge ordered him to call twelve men. He instructed the men to take a seat in the jury box when their name was called. As each man was called, he would rise and walk to the jury box and take a seat in the chairs provided for the group. After the twelve chairs were filled, the clerk looked toward the Judge and announced the jury had been set.

Following the Judge's interrogation of the jury, he invited the prosecutor to question the jury to determine whether or not they were acceptable to the prosecution.

The prosecutor began questioning the different members of the jury to try to determine if any of them knew the defendant or if any of them had served under him during the war. When several admitted that they knew Arch, and several stated they had served either with him or under him, the Judge interrupted and stated that knowing Arch or serving with him or under him in the Confederate army would not be accepted as cause for dismissal. He justified this reasoning by saying that if those who knew Arch, or served with or under him in the army during the war were dismissed, there wouldn't be enough men left to hold the trial and he fully intended to hold this trial that day.

Looking sorely disappointed, the prosecutor announced that he would accept the jury as seated. Turning to the defense attorney, the Judge asked if he had any questions of the jury. He responded that he was quite satisfied with the jury and had no questions to ask.

Now the trial began. The prosecutor first called the sheriff to testify as to what had transpired on the day before the courthouse burned.

Following this lead, the sheriff testified that on the day the courthouse burned, a trial had been held and that Arch had been convicted of killing a bull belonging to Samson Roddenberry. Following the conviction, the Judge had ordered Arch to pay Mr. Roddenberry the amount of ten dollars in damages for the bull he had killed. He then told that Arch had paid the ten dollars with a bright, shiny gold ten-dollar piece. He noted that following the payment of the fine, Arch had appeared to be extremely mad about the fine, stating that the Judge knew that a damn cow was worth only about fifty-cents and that he would have to sell twenty cows to pay the fine. He further stated that when Arch left the courtroom he (Arch) had been mad as hell. He did not appear to be mad about the verdict because he readily admitted to killing the bull. It seemed instead that he was mad about the fine that had been imposed. He had vocally stated his displeasure and the sheriff stated that he had been glad when Arch had helped Duck into the wagon and left. Knowing of Arch's violent temper when mad, he had been afraid someone might incite him with some statement and possibly get hurt.

When the defense attorney cross-examined the sheriff he asked, "Sheriff, after Arch left, did you see him again that day or that night?"

The sheriff answered, "No, I didn't see Arch again until my deputy and I went to arrest him several weeks later."

"Did Arch give you or your deputy any trouble when he was arrested?"

"No, he appeared to be surprised when we told him our mission and only asked if we would permit him to bathe and change clothes. We allowed him to do these things and then he accompanied us to the county seat and was locked up in the jail."

"When he was bathing and changing clothes was he visible to you or your deputy?"

"No," the sheriff said. "We had no reason to think he would escape. Where in the hell do you think he would have gone?"

"Did you handcuff him when you carried him to jail?"

"No," was the sheriff's reply.

"Why would I want to handcuff someone I have known for many years and who has never given us any trouble?"

Noting that he didn't have a witness who would help the case against Arch, the prosecutor turned to the defense attorney and said, "Your witness." The defense attorney said he had no questions of the sheriff and he was dismissed from the stand.

The next witness called was the young deputy who, after being sworn in, testified that he had been curious regarding the cause of the fire and he had looked about the area of the courthouse the next morning afterwards. Some distance away in a clump of trees, he had found a kerosene can with the logo of John Raker's store on it. He said, "I couldn't understand someone throwing away a new kerosene can, so I started asking questions. I learned from Mr. Raker that he had sold a kerosene can to Arch the afternoon before the fire. He couldn't swear the can I showed him was the can he had sold Arch, but it looked exactly like it. I then talked to Mr. Aligood later that afternoon and he told me he had sat on his porch that faces the courthouse the afternoon before the fire, smoking his pipe. When I asked if he had seen anything unusual, he had said he hadn't seen anything that he could think of. When I asked if he had seen anyone he said, "Yes, I saw Arch." I then asked what he had been doing and he told me Arch was walking toward the courthouse with what appeared to be a kerosene can. He assumed that he was going to get his horse that was tied to the hitching rail at the rear of the courthouse. He had thought he was on his way home.

While the prosecutor was questioning the deputy, those in the audience were amused to see Arch reach beneath the table where he sat and retrieve a kerosene can exactly like the one the prosecutor had shown the jury earlier.

After the prosecutor completed his examination of the witness, he indicated to the defense attorney that it was now his turn to question the deputy. Mr. Long arose and asked if Mr. Aligood had said he had seen Arch enter the courthouse fence. The deputy said he hadn't asked that question, but if it was important they could ask Uncle Pat because he was present in the courtroom.

Next the prosecutor called Mr. John Raker. After he was sworn in, he was asked if the kerosene can the deputy had shown him was the one he sold Arch the afternoon before the fire. As he looked toward the table where Arch sat with a kerosene can exactly like the one the prosecutor was holding, Mr. Raker said he couldn't be sure since over the years he had sold several hundred cans exactly like it.

The defense attorney declined to ask any questions of this witness.

Now the prosecutor called Mr. Patrick Aligood, and when he was sworn in, the Judge admonished him to tell the truth. Rising from his seat and standing directly in front of the Judge, he pointed his finger at the Judge and said, "Young man, I always tell the truth regardless of the consequences, but if I thought that telling a lie would help this man who is being tried, I would never tell the truth again as long as I live. No man has ever been a truer friend and as my commanding officer during the time I was in the Confederate army, and the subsequent period afterwards, he saved my life on numerous occasions. So don't expect me to testify to anything that might harm Arch."

The courtroom was quiet for a few moments and after Mr. Aligood had returned to his seat in the witness box, the Judge, looking embarrassed, turned and looked directly at Mr. Aligood. He said, "I only want you to tell what you know about this case and by my comments I did not have any intentions of impugning your integrity in any way, or to imply you would be anything but honest. I wish to apologize, and I trust you will accept my apology."

Mr. Aligood responded by saying, "Your apology is accepted."

The prosecutor began by asking the witness if the testimony of the previous witness, the deputy, represented the conversation he had with him.

The old man thought for a few moments and then replied,

"The deputy's testimony represented the exact conversation the two of us had regarding the afternoon before the fire."

Next the prosecutor asked if he had seen Arch enter the courtyard or if he had seen Arch mount his horse and ride away.

Pat thought a few moments and then replied, "I cain't say what he did because it was about the time my wife called and asked if I would come inside and churn the butter. When I finished the churning it was dark and I soon went to bed. Sometime later, I was awakened by a gun shot and loud screams. When I awoke I could see a bright light through my window. I quickly realized the courthouse was burning and it was one hell of a fire."

The prosecutor recognized this witness wasn't going to be much help. Turning to the defense attorney, he said, "Your witness."

Mr. Long declined to cross-examine Mr. Aligood.

The prosecutor then announced that he rested his case.

Mr. Long arose and announced that he would not call any defense witnesses.

The Judge then announced, "We are going to take a thirty-minute break and when we return for your closing arguments you both will make them brief. I never could stand long winded attorneys."

Following the break the prosecutor spoke to the jury at great length, pointing out that while the case as presented was largely circumstantial, he believed the facts, when tied together in the manner in which he had presented them to the jury, left little doubt as to what happened and who caused the fire. He then went to the table. Turning to the Judge he said, "The state rests its case."

Now the Judge called for the defense attorney to make his rebuttal. When Mr. Long arose, he looked at Arch and began by saying, "Gentlemen of the jury, you have sat here today very patiently and my comments won't keep you here much longer.

I believe the courthouse did burn, but the charges against this man have not been proven in this courtroom. I ask you to consider all the facts carefully and then return the only verdict that can be reached based on the information that has been presented here today, and that verdict should be, *Not Guilty*."

"Most of you have known this man for considerable periods of your life and I am sure you have found him to be an honorable man who spent six long years of his life fighting for our lost cause. This man, who by his diligent, devoted service, rose from the rank of private to become a commissioned officer in the Confederate army. He was released from a Yankee prison where he had been placed because he refused to pledge allegiance to a Yankee government. He chose to be incarcerated in a Yankee army prison along with the old man who sat in the witness box last and another comrade only to be released six months later in the north. They were without any transportation or funds and this forced them to walk from the state of New Jersey to Atlanta, Georgia, a distance of several hundred miles. There they eventually acquired transportation and returned to their homes. Not one person appeared in this courtroom to testify that his man had caused anyone harm without just cause. Now I ask you to exercise your duty and find him not guilty of the charges that have been brought against him and to allow him to return to his home to be with is wife and their children so that he can continue to provide for them in the same manner he has in the past. I thank you for your attention and patience."

He then returned to the defense table and sat down by Arch.

The courtroom was quiet for a brief period following Mr. Long's speech to the jury. After a few moments, the Judge began his instructions to the jury. He ordered them to retire and begin their deliberations. They were instructed to render a verdict on the evidence that was presented in the courtroom that day.

Turning to the spectators he announced that the court would be at ease. When the Judge made this announcement, much shuffling and moving about began, and conversations between the many people could be heard. From across the courtroom, the booming voice of the giant of a man Amos could he heard when he arose and called loudly across the room, "Zeke, what is the verdict going to be?"

The little man Zeke stood up and stretched. Looking toward Amos he replied, "Why hell Amos, nine members of that jury are veterans, so there is little doubt what the verdict will be."

The defense attorney, Mr. Long, was still sitting at the defense table. He turned toward Zeke with a big grin on his face and winked at him, indicating his approval of the conclusion that had been made by the little man.

Shortly, the bailiff approached the Judge and indicated the jury had reached a verdict. The Judge called the court back into session and instructed the bailiff to return the jury to the courtroom. As they filed back in, they all looked in the direction of the defense table where Arch and Mr. Long sat. This was a good sign that the verdict they reached would be in the defendant's favor.

When the jury was seated, the Judge turned to the foreman and asked, "Mr. Foreman, has the jury reached a verdict?"

"The foreman of the jury responded by saying, "We have, your Honor."

"What is the verdict?" asked the Judge.

Looking toward the defendant, the foreman announced the verdict as "Not guilty."

When these words were spoken a cheer went up in the courtroom. Looking across the room, you could see a smile appear on the young deputy's face. He was just as pleased with the verdict as the veterans who now were crowding around Arch, offering their congratulations.

When Arch and Duck, along with Pat Aligood, left the courthouse, it was growing late in the afternoon. They went to the hotel nearby to find a place of lodging for the night. The train had already left going south and it would be late the next day before any transportation would be available to carry them home.

Following their supper at the hotel dining room, they retired. After they had gone to bed, Duck said, "I told you that temper would get you in trouble, didn't I?"

"Yes," he answered. "I learned my lessons. I won't go around killing any more of Samson's bulls unless they get in my corn patch, and I won't burn down any more courthouses."

With this comment he turned over and went to sleep, a big smile on his face.

24

Epilogue

One morning, several years later and two days after Christmas, the young deputy, now the elected sheriff of the county, heard disturbing news. A man came by the Sheriff's Office that morning to tell him that Arch died the morning following Christmas. The young sheriff immediately saddled his horse and rode the several miles to Arch's farm to express his sorrow to the widow and the five boys that had been left fatherless.

Duck was impressed that the young sheriff was so thoughtful and she thanked him for his concern. When asked what she intended to do now that she had no husband to provide for the family, Duck answered quietly, "Why, I'll take these boys and run this farm just like their daddy did."

Time passed and the boys grew up to be men. Their father would have been proud of his offspring as they prospered and became known as honorable men of their community. Subsequent generations served their country in war and peace becoming law enforcement officers, lawyers and members of the court.